A WALLFLOWER'S CHRISTMAS KISS

A WALLFLOWER'S CHRISTMAS KISS

CONNECTED BY A KISS 3

DAWN BROWER

MONARCHAL GLENN PRESS

CONTENTS

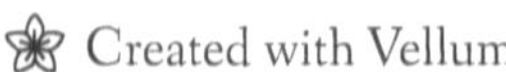 Created with Vellum

WISHING FOR A KISS

The shooting star awaits a wish
It's alluring and quite roguish
The flame is hot, as hot as fire
In the dark, rife with desire
Close your eyes, wish for bliss
And experience a scoundrel's kiss...

PROLOGUE

A fire blazed in the hearth and along with several sconces of candles kept the room aglow. The window was glazed over with ice, as little Lady Juliette Brooks stared outside. The velvet black sky sparkled with stars twinkling down with heavenly light. A luminous streak filled the sky as a star shot across the darkness. Lady Juliette's heart beat heavily in her chest. This was her chance to make the wish she'd been carrying inside of her for so long. There was only one thing her nine year old heart desired more than anything in the world. It was to always have her best friend by her side. She couldn't imagine a life where he was no longer in it.

"What is so interesting?"

Juliette turned and met Lord Grayson Abbot's, the future Duke of Kissinger's, gaze. Her family estate bordered Kissinger Castle the ducal estate. Her father was the Earl of Riverdale. Every Christmastide their families came together to celebrate. Not that Grayson and Juliette ever needed a reason to spend time together. As long as she remembered he'd always been by her side. He was as patient, kind, and loyal as a twelve year old boy could be. She imagined he'd grow up to be the hero every girl swooned over.

"I made a wish on a shooting star," Juliette said.

Grayson peeked over her shoulder and stared at the night sky. "I don't see anything."

"Don't be silly," she retorted. "Shooting stars dissolve as fast as they make an appearance. I'm sure my wish sent it on its way."

Grayson stood behind her his gaze focused on the darkness outside the window. Juliette wasn't used to his silence—it was almost crushing, and unbearable to withstand. After a moment he stepped back and put some distance between them. Something was wrong—horribly so. He was distancing himself from her. What had she done?

"What did you wish for?"

Finally he spoke to her, but it didn't ease her

concern. He held himself stiff and distant. She didn't like this side of him. What happened to the friend who was always willing to have fun and play silly games with her? She missed that Grayson and wanted him back. This boy in front of her was almost a stranger.

"I can't tell you or it won't come true."

He tilted his head and a stray lock of his dark hair fell over his forehead. He sighed. His blue eyes were almost as glacial as the ice outside. "I hate to break your heart," he said with feigned concern. "But you should know wishes never come true. They're a falsehood best left to story books."

"They are not," Juliette exclaimed. "Why are you being so mean?"

This was not her Grayson. Her friend would never be so cruel. What had happened since she'd last seen him? It had been less than a sennight. She'd found him at the pond separating their estate. He'd been sitting on the frozen water and staring down at it as if he expected to find the answers to all his questions. He'd been quiet then, but not like this.

"I've coddled you long enough don't you think?" He crossed his arms across his chest. "I'm growing up and you're a silly little girl."

Juliette's bottom lip stuck out as a full on pout

formed. Tears pooled at the corner of her eyes. Big droplets fell down her cheeks. What had she done to make him act thusly? She lifted her hand and wiped away the wetness from her face. If he was going to be a surly brutish nitwit than she had better things to do with her time—and being called a silly little girl didn't top her list. "It is sad when I think about it," she replied.

"What is?" he asked.

"That I was foolish enough to waste my wish on you." She stomped away from him and left him to stare out the window. A friend that belittled you was no friend indeed, and Juliette didn't need one who'd do something so dastardly.

GRAYSON ABBOT STARED at the entrance of the sitting room. He should go after her and explain why he was being so churlish. It wasn't her fault he had to go away. He wanted to make sure she was able to make it on her own. He wouldn't be around much longer to protect her. Soon he'd be at Eton and would only see her on holidays. Father had informed him of the plan a sennight ago. He should have expected it. All young lords either went to Harrow or

Eton to start their education. A tutor could only do so much to ensure an heir was properly taught. Grayson already devoured every book his tutor had put in front of him. He thirsted for more knowledge, but he hadn't realized what that desire would lead to. He'd have to leave Juliette behind, and there wasn't a thing he could do to change that. She'd been his only friend for so long he couldn't imagine a day where he'd not be able to see her.

He should apologize, and yet he stayed still as if frozen in place.

Juliette wouldn't understand. She'd think he was abandoning her, and her heart would surely break. She'd wished on a shooting star and still believed there was a possibility it could come true. How could he have mocked her so cruelly? He sighed and forced his feet to move. The sooner he found her the quicker he'd be able to grovel at her feet.

He found her in the billiards room pushing the balls across the table. They rolled across the smooth surface and hit the other side with a soft thunk. "If your father finds you in here you'll be punished."

"I don't care," she replied mulishly. "Christmas is ruined anyway. I'd be happy to stay in my room for the rest of the festivities. At least then I wouldn't have to see you."

Grayson sighed. Why did his heart melt whenever he was around her? This little girl had meant so much to him for so long... Her raven-black tresses spilled around her shoulders in soft curls, and her blue-green eyes usually sparkling with mischief were now filled with misery. That was his fault. He'd ruined Christmastide for her, and it wasn't going to improve much with his apology.

"Please forgive me," he coaxed. "I didn't mean to take out my concerns on you."

She perked up at his words. Her eyes were brighter and some of the sadness left them, but the evidence of her gloom still bloomed on her barely dried cheeks. "What is bothering you?" She moved to his side. "I'll help if I can."

She would do anything for him as he was well aware. That is what friends did for each other. Soon they'd have too much distance between them, and friendship between a lord and a lady wasn't done. It was best that he cut the ties now and left her to grow up without him by her side. His father explained he couldn't have a friend like Lady Juliette if he was at Eton. He'd be a laughing stock and be twice as miserable.

"There's nothing you can do for me poppet," he

said. "I'm to go to school and won't be living next door any longer."

"No," she said. "You can't leave I won't let you."

He pressed his lips together and slowly shook his head. "I must. I'll be a duke someday and I need to be educated so I can properly run my estates."

Juliette stuck her nose in the air and folded her arms over her chest. "That's not happening for a very long time. Your father is the duke, and he doesn't have to send you away."

"Oh, Jules," he said with sadness. "I want to go."

That was the hardest part for him. He craved more than knowledge. He wanted friends who were not little girls who lived next door. Boys his own age and who shared similar interests. Juliette was his past and he had a future he must plan for. Staying cooped up in his father's estate with only a tutor and a mere girl as his only friend wouldn't aide him in his goals.

"I thought as much," she said glumly. "I'd hoped it was against your will."

His lips twitched. Juliette always did manage to surprise him. She was only nine years old, but sometimes acted as if she was on the verge of her come out. He supposed it had a lot to do with their isolation. Neither one of them was allowed to play with the servant's children, nor were there any other children of their rank around to fill in the gaps. They'd been forced to grow up much too young.

"It won't be forever," he promised. "I'll be home on holidays and school breaks. We'll see each other again."

Juliette sat down on a nearby chair. "It won't be the same."

What could he do to make her understand? Nothing. She didn't need him to explain any of it. Her gaze said it all. She was aware of why he had to go away—it just wasn't to her liking. "In time you'll forget about me. You'll go to finishing school and learn how to become a proper lady. Then you'll have your come out and find a husband. I'll be a distant memory, a foolish boy who was once a neighboring playmate."

She shook her head. "I could never forget you."

Sadly he believed that was true. A part of him didn't want her to. This might very well be their last Christmastide together, though, and he didn't want to waste it with melancholy thoughts. There had to be something he could do to bring a smile back to her face. An idea took root and he decided to try it.

"I don't want to leave you sad," he said. "I have a present for you. Would you like it now?"

"Oh, yes," Juliette bobbed her head. "Please."

"Give me a moment to retrieve it," he explained. "Meet me in the sitting room. I don't want you to be punished if you're found in here." He couldn't help his need to protect her. As long as he was around her —she'd always come first. It had been ingrained in him for so long it was a habit he had trouble breaking.

"Very well," she agreed.

They both exited the billiards room. Juliette headed toward the sitting room, and Grayson headed toward his guest chamber. During Christmastide his family spent half of it at Riverdale Park and Juliette's family spent the other half at Kissinger Castle. The gift he'd purchased for Juliette, Grayson had always planned on giving her in private. His father would berate him if he was aware of what he'd had commissioned. Juliette would love it though. He quickly retrieved the small box and tucked it inside his pocket. Satisfied it was secured; Grayson left his room and toward the sitting room. He found Juliette staring out the window once again. This was his second chance to redo his earlier blunder. He'd not make the same mistake again.

"Any more shooting stars?"

She giggled. "No I think that was the only one we're going to ever see."

"I don't know. One day we might be lucky enough to see another."

What boy of twelve had ever looked at a girl and knew she was the only one who'd ever own his heart? Grayson gazed down at her in wonderment. He was being absurd. Juliette was a mere nine years old. He'd not be able to tell the woman she'd become in the next decade. They had a lot of growing up to do and may not suit after they reached their majority.

"Did you bring my gift?"

He reached into his pocket and withdrew the small box. His hand was fisted tightly around the sharp corners. When he'd purchased it he'd believed Juliette would love it. What if he was wrong? There was one way to find out. With much trepidation he stretched out his arm and offered it to her. She clapped gleefully and tore open the box.

And then remained silent for several heart wrenching moments...

"Oh Gray." She sighed. "It's so lovely."

She picked up the delicate locket and flipped it open...inside nestled a tiny portrait of him. "If you don't like it you can put—"

"Don't even consider finishing what you were about to say. This is the best gift you could've ever given me." She kept it tightly in her grasp. "Whenever I'm sad you're gone, I can look at it and remember you."

He let out a sigh of relief. So he'd not misjudged, but a part of him wondered if he was only delaying the inevitable. His job was to encourage her to move on, and this wasn't achieving that goal.

"I'm glad you like it."

"Can you promise me something?" she asked.

Grayson wanted to promise her the world. He'd lay it at her feet if it kept her smiling and as happy as she was in that moment. "Of course," he said emphatically.

"If I ever need you, you'll be there for me." She gazed up into his eyes with trust shining through. "No matter what it takes."

Grayson opened his mouth to respond, but wasn't sure if he was capable of it. What she asked should be an easy thing to agree to, but he feared it wouldn't be so simple. Nothing ever was where promises were concerned. He'd hate to break it, and in turn the part of her he'd always adored. Her faith in him was unwavering and a little unnerving. He feared he'd never live up to her expectations. Perhaps he was over thinking things and should give her what she desired. Chances were they'd not see much of each other after this Christmastide either way. So he gave in and agreed.

He nodded. "I promise I'll always be there. You can depend on me to do whatever is necessary to aid you."

Grayson vowed he'd keep that promise, even it cost him everything...

CHAPTER 1

Could her life possible get any worse? Lady Juliette Brooks fell on her bed and let out a frustrated sigh. She should be able to go out in society, and find a husband. Her only desire was to escape her father's house and start a family of her own. Truthfully, she'd settle for escaping alone—her stepmother Eloise was the bane of her existence.

If only Mother hadn't died... Everything would be so different, and Juliette wouldn't have had her first season cut short. She'd not been out a fortnight before tragedy struck her family. There'd been no time to find proper suitors, and even if a gentleman had caught her eye no one noticed her. She'd made no friends, barely conversed with a soul, and found the sidelines much to her liking. At least that last part is what she kept telling herself. She'd never imagined she'd be a wallflower watching all the other ladies twirling around the ballroom and laughing with enjoyment.

None of it had gone as she'd planned, and the one person she'd wanted to see hadn't bothered in too many years to count. After the mourning period ended, Juliette fully believed she'd rejoin society and the marriage mart. Nothing of the sort happened. Instead, her father had found Eloise and promptly married her. The new Lady Riverdale wanted nothing to do with Juliette. She'd not commissioned any new gowns and made no plans to re-launch her in society. Father had been too smitten with his new countess to bother with Juliette. She might as well have become invisible as much notice as those around her paid to her life. After a while she'd rather liked no one bothering her. She buried herself in books and embraced the life of spinsterhood. Why bother with marriage when she had all she needed at her father's home. Who needed new frocks when her old ones could be redesigned and altered? At least that was what Juliette kept telling herself.

Until her little brother was born she kept to herself and did as she pleased. With father finally having his heir he suddenly realized he had another child. A daughter he'd neglected, and tossed aside for his new family. Juliette suspected Eloise prompted his sudden attention. She'd been eyeing her warily for a while, and made no secret she'd wanted her gone. So years after she should have had a second come-out Juliette's season was being planned.

At five and twenty she'd let that dream go.

She couldn't dawdle in her room much longer. Her father had summoned her presence in his study. What he wanted she could only guess, but ever since the maid had informed her of the request, Juliette's stomach had been a flutter of unease. Slowly she strolled down the stairs and headed in the direction of her father's study. She paused outside the entrance and listened.

"Lord Payne will make a wonderful husband for Juliette," her step-mother cooed. "At her advanced age she has little choices, and a viscount is more than she could hope for."

Juliette opened her mouth as a silent gasp slipped out. She lifted her hands and placed both over her face. Surely Eloise wasn't that cruel. Did she not know the viscount's reputation? He was rumored to beat servants and small children. What he considered his could be dealt with as he pleased. He'd not treat a wife any differently. She'd rather die than tie herself to such a man. Her father wouldn't agree—he couldn't...

"He does possess a good fortune," her father replied. "His estates are flourishing, he's neither given to excessive drink nor gambling."

Juliette's heart fell at her father's words. There was more to a man then how much he imbibed or gambled. She did not want to be saddled with a poor man, but if given the choice she'd rather live in a hovel than be beaten every day. That was what her fate would be if they forced her to marry Lord Payne. Juliette stepped closer and peaked inside the slit in the door.

"He isn't too old for her either." Her step-mother sat down in her father's lap. "She'll still be able to have a family of her own. Juliette should know the joys of motherhood. It's a good match. When Lord Payne arrives in a few days to sign the marriage contract, your daughter will be well taken care of."

Juliette clenched her fingers together into a tight fist. How dare she? All she cared about was herself. She saw Juliette as competition, and was doing everything in her power to get rid of her. What was the hurry? The spring season wasn't that far away, only mere months. Why was Eloise forcing the issue so soon? Did Juliette not deserve a choice?

She couldn't take it anymore. If she had to listen a second longer she'd lose the contents of her stomach. This plan of Eloise's must be stopped. Juliette eased the door open and cleared her throat. "Ahem, father, you asked to see me."

Eloise and her father were locked in a passionate embrace. A gag rose in her throat at the sight. She should be used to it by now, but it always sat uneasily inside of her. Her new step-mother was an usurper in her life. She'd never take the place of her mother, and she'd never stop missing the woman's love. The new countess while a beauty, was selfish and vain.

Eloise stood and crossed the room to meet her. "Please, come in dear. There's much your father and I wish to discuss with you."

She bet they did. They were about to unload a bunch of misery on her she'd not felt—well not since her mother's death, and before that the abandonment of her only friend. What was one more momentous bout of melancholy to add to her list? This one would be the last if she had anything to say about it.

"Oh?" she raised an eyebrow. "Please continue."

"Why don't you have a seat dear." Her father gestured toward a chair. "There is much we have to tell you."

Juliette did as her father bid and sat in a chair.

Her father's study had been one of her favorite places as a child. At least in their London townhouse. Her favorite place to be was Riverdale Park, but she'd not been to her family's country seat in years. Not since her mother's death. Her father had chosen to remain in London instead of visiting a place of happier times. It had brought nothing but pain to him, and then he'd met Eloise. The new countess abhorred country life and begged him to remain in London. A part of Juliette longed for Christmastides of the past. When Riverdale Park was filled with visitors and the festivities lasted days.

London was rather ugly and drab in comparison.

"After careful deliberation," her father began. "I've come to a decision regarding your future."

"You have?" Juliette tilted her head. "Am I to shop for new gowns? I do need some current attire for the upcoming season."

If her father was aware of her penchant for listening at doors he'd punish her for her insolence. For now she'd play along with his news, and then afterward she'd make a plan of escape. She'd not be marrying Lord Payne.

"I'm afraid that won't be necessary," Eloise said. Her lips tilted up smugly. "You won't be having a season as planned."

"I'm not?" She widened her eyes in feigned shock. "Why? Has something happened?"

She wanted to wipe that smug smile off of the countess's face. She believed she'd won, but in time she'd realize she hadn't. Eloise wanted her gone, and she'd get her wish one way or the other.

Her father's gruff voice interrupted her musings. "I've been in talks with Viscount Payne. He's interested in marriage to you, and it's my belief it will be a good match. He'll be here in less than a sennight to go over the marriage contracts."

Juliette clenched her fingers together. She could not give into the desire to scream. It wouldn't do if she showed any emotion. If she did Eloise would use it against her, and in turn drive her father in the direction she wanted him to go.

"Father," she began. "I appreciate you looking out for me, but marriage to Lord Payne is not something I desire. While I don't blame mother—I did miss out on my season. I'd prefer to at least have a small season." She smiled encouragingly. "A choice at least in husbands."

Please let him agree. She couldn't marry Lord Payne. Hadn't she already paid the ultimate price? No, she supposed not. That would include the loss of her life, and that price was too high... She had too much she wanted to do with her life.

"I'm afraid I can't humor you, child." Juliette almost snorted. She'd not been a child in years, but perhaps her father would always see her as such. "Lord Payne insists that I sign the contract now or not at all."

That worked perfectly as far as she was concerned. She didn't want to marry the viscount, and no amount of coaxing would change her mind. "I see," she replied. "That would be a grave loss for sure..." She paused and considered her words. "But surely there would be others willing to marry me. Ties to the Riverdale line aren't anything to scoff at."

"You're correct," he agreed. "However the same could be said about Lord Payne. It's a good match and I'm not changing my mind. The contracts will be signed before the end of Christmastide, and you'll be married after the new year once the bans have been read."

Juliette gulped down the lump in her throat. There was no reasoning with her father. He was fully ensconced in Eloise's control. She was pulling his strings, and therefore she presumed Juliette's. Well the countess would see in time that no one would ever control her. Before the day was out she'd be gone, and out of their lives.

"As you desire," Juliette nodded demurely. She couldn't give them even a hint of what she had planned. "May I be excused?"

"Yes dear," her father said. "When Lord Payne arrives I want you to be on your best behavior."

"Of course father," she replied. "I'm always the proper lady." Not that he'd felt the need to send her to finishing school. Her father could be quite miserly with funds at times. He'd believed it wasn't necessary to spend a fortune on schooling a mere girl. The earl left her deportment lessons to her mother and governess.

She bowed her head and then stood to leave. When she reached the entrance her step-mother's voice made her pause. "Juliette dear," Eloise said. "I'll escort you to your room. There is something I wish to speak with you about."

Drat. What did the woman want? Hadn't she done enough to ruin her life? Juliette turned and met Eloise's gaze. "I look forward to it." She waited for the countess to join her. They strolled side by side down the hall in silence. When was she going to say something?

"I hope you won't put up a fuss about the

marriage," Lady Riverdale began. "Lord Payne will make a good husband for you."

Juliette bit down on her bottom lip. A drop of blood trickled into her mouth from the impact. If she said what was truly in her heart Lady Eloise would make things much worse for her, and escape near impossible. For now she must appear as biddable as possible.

"I look forward to starting a family of my own. It's what I've always wanted."

"Good. I'm glad we were able to arrange an advantageous match for you."

They reached Juliette's chamber. Thank God. She could bid Eloise good night and start her plan of escape. "Good night Lady Riverdale." She always addressed Eloise formally. It was what Eloise preferred. In her thoughts though she called her anything she wanted. The countess nodded her head dismissing Juliette.

After she was inside she locked the door and pulled out her reticule. She'd not be able to take much with her, but there were a few items she refused to leave behind. Most of it was sentimental in value as she had little worth. The little bit of pin money she had would have to do. She hoped it wouldn't matter either way.

If he kept the promise he made her all those years ago, she'd not worry for anything. He was her last hope, and if he refused her she'd have no choice but to follow her father's dictate. She prayed it wouldn't come to that. It was a sad day indeed when her life depended upon the Duke of Kissinger—desolate rake, debaucher of anything in a skirt, and a reprobate of the highest level. The scandal sheets took pleasure in outlining many of his exploits.

CHAPTER 2

Grayson Abbot, the Duke of Kissinger lounged in his study sipping a fine brandy. He'd vacated his good friend Christian, the Marquis of Knightly's townhouse earlier that evening. He enjoyed the company of good friends, and the townhouse definitely boasted a few of them, but he'd also been a little depressed watching them bask in their happiness. An emotion that had eluded him for more years than he recalled. No that wasn't entirely true, he could pinpoint the exact moment when it had been ripped from his life.

He blamed his father for it.

Grayson lifted the goblet of brandy in a mock toast. "This is to you good ole' dad." He downed the remaining contents in one gulp. It was more than the bastard deserved.

After he'd gone away to Eton he'd not been permitted to return home. It was his father's brand of tough love. The previous duke hadn't liked his growing friendship with the Earl of Riverdale's daughter. Boys don't have girls as playmates—at least according to the dictates of his late father.

His death freed Grayson in so many ways, but his fate had been set long before that blessed event. Instead of giving into his father's demands of education and strict structure of running the estates, Grayson took a different path. One that led to debauchery of every kind imaginable. It was an endeavor he took very seriously. Decadence, followed by wickedness, could only be done right when he threw himself into it whole heartedly. He'd not regretted one moment of it. At that point in his life he'd already lost anything worth keeping, and all he'd held dear would forever be out of reach.

"Pardon me, Your Grace," his butler, Burrows, said. "A visitor is here to see you."

Grayson growled at the announcement. "Who the bloody hell would come here at this late hour?" All of his friends were still at Knightly's townhouse. He'd left to escape their sickly outpouring of joy.

This was unacceptable. Was it too much to ask for peace and quiet in his own home?

"It's a lady, Your Grace."

Well, well, that was something different entirely. A woman was exactly what he needed. He rubbed his chin and considered who it could be. Lady Danvers had taken an interest in him when he ran into her at the opera, or it could be the lead in the opera... The list was endless. He liked to keep his options open and never committed to any one woman.

"By all means show the lady in," he ordered. "A lady is always welcome to keep me company." Burrows remained still inside the doorway. Why hadn't he gone to retrieve the woman already. Grayson was excited to see which fair beauty had the daring to grace his home uninvited. "Why are you still standing there? Go fetch her. It's not good to keep a lady waiting. They don't like that sort of thing." Unless it built up passion and desire, then the screams were well worth it.

Burrows cleared his throat. "It's not that kind of lady, Your Grace."

His butler was well acquainted with Grayson's proclivities. If he said the woman in question wasn't his usual sort—that could only mean one thing. It was an innocent he wouldn't have the pleasure of ravishing, that is, unless he planned on being caught by the parson's trap. Something he had no intention of ever doing. He didn't care if he never had an heir to pass his title down to. The damned thing could go to whatever distant cousin was next in line.

"In that case," he replied. "Please inform the chit I'm not at home to visitors." A part of him wondered who it was, but he couldn't allow himself the honor of finding out. She was better off not entering any further than the foyer. Just being in his home could tatter her reputation. He was doing her a favor by denying her an audience.

"When it's clear you very much are?" A feminine voice filled the room.

Grayson sighed. She wasn't going to be denied anything apparently. It was too late to save her from herself. Very well, he'd deal with her and then send her on her way. He turned and sucked in a breath momentarily stunned. A silhouette of pure beauty greeted him. Her midnight tresses were wound up and bound neatly into an elegant chignon. His fingers itched to unwind it and see it flow over her luscious curves. All of this and he'd still not seen her face. When she finally turned to meet his gaze he lost all ability to breathe. Those sea-green eyes kept him riveted in place. He should stand and greet her but his body refused to function. She was the last person he expected or wanted to enter his home.

"What no words?" She raised an eyebrow. "And I thought you were noted as the witty duke amongst the *ton*. I must say, I'm rather disappointed."

Grayson drank in the sight of her. He wanted to remember her as she stood before him for the rest of his days. She was glorious, proud, and fearless. "Didn't your father teach you better than to enter the lion's den?" He lifted a brow mockingly. "You could very well get eaten alive."

Her lips tilted at the corner. "I rather like my chances." She moved further into the room. "After all I've tamed a lion before."

"There's a difference between a young cub, and a full grown male, Jules," he explained. "One is more docile and willing to cuddle. The adult wants to be petted—in other ways." He stood up and gazed directly into her eyes. "A bite can be pleasurable or...." Grayson crossed over to her side and leaned down, whispering in her ear, "or painful depending on your preference."

Juliette took a deep breath but remained where she stood. He'd give her that much. She'd always been a stubborn girl, and apparently she'd not grown out of that trait. If she didn't take a step back soon he'd be forced to make a choice. Either he pulled her into his arms and kissed her the way he craved or he put distance between them respecting her innocence. It was a hard decision and warred deep inside him, but he did what was best for her. Turned out that some things were ingrained. Protecting her had always been his first instinct.

"If you're done trying to intimidate me, I have something I wish to discuss with you."

"I need a drink," he said ignoring her statement. He headed toward his decanter of brandy and filled his glass to the top. If he were to make it through this interview he'd need a little, no make that a lot, of liquid courage. Dealing with Lady Juliette Brooks was something he'd hope to avoid for the rest of his life. He'd done her a disservice by befriending her all those years ago.

"It seems you've had plenty already." She scrunched her nose up with displeasure. "Must you pour more down your throat?"

He lifted a brow. "One doesn't pour fine brandy down their throat," he mocked. "It's sipped, savored, and drawn out to enhance the enticing flavor. Good liquor is as delectable as a woman. A fine one deserves slow intricate attention to thoroughly appreciate it."

She sighed. "All you had to do was say *no*." Juliette placed her hands on her hips. "You can dispense with your rake rhetoric. I don't have time for it."

Just like that she dismissed everything he'd said as nonsense. Why wasn't any of it working on her? Other ladies swooned when he spoke with such wickedness. But not Lady Juliette, no, she brushed it aside as nonsense. How was he to scare her off if she didn't take a word he said seriously?

"Would you like a drink?" Grayson gestured toward the decanter. "It appears you could use a stiff one." He wiggled his eyebrows suggestively.

She glanced at the brandy and then back at him. "Yes. Please pour me a glass. It's been a tiresome day, and it would help me relax."

It was the last thing he expected to come out of her mouth. Maybe he didn't know her as well as he'd thought. It had been a long time since they'd had an actual conversation. Sure, he'd been kept informed, but that wasn't the same as being a part of her life. Keeping his distance had seemed like a good idea. Now that she was in front of him, and more beautiful than he recalled, his error was clear.

He poured her brandy and handed it to her. "Why haven't you married?"

Her mother's death had stopped her season early, but that shouldn't have prevented her from having several potential suitors. Why hadn't she had another season after her mourning period ended? Was her grief that great? She should be married, happy, and a mother of several children by now. It had been what he'd prayed for.

The tidbits he'd garnered over the years told him the little details. Riverdale, along with his daughter, remained in London, the earl remarried and had his heir, and Lady Juliette was fast becoming a spinster who rarely went out in society. He didn't quite understand why.

"No one wants me. I was a wallflower, and then I had no season at all."

He found that hard to believe. Who wouldn't want her? She was more beautiful than any woman he'd ever known. Perhaps he saw her differently, but he doubted it. The small glimpse of her he'd had at her come out ball had been enough for him to see how lovely she'd become. It was the last sight he'd had of her before he ran to the nearest gaming hell and drowned his sorrows in a bottle of brandy. He barely recalled much after that. Somehow he'd managed to find his way home and had planned to spend the night alone.

"They're all fools," he said. "None of them deserve you." He swallowed half the contents of his glass.

"Yes, well, you weren't there. So how would you know?"

It pained him to see the hurt filling her eyes. She glanced down and played with the rim of her glass. Grayson could tell her he'd gone, but what good would that do? He'd not been able to stay. His father had still been alive then and held him in check. Soon after that the damage had been done and he'd found solace in becoming a man his father despised.

"Right you are." He lifted his glass and saluted her. "Your skill at putting me in my place has always been superior."

Juliette lifted her glass and took a long unlady-like swig. She sat on a nearby settee and settled her glass on the table next to it. "I'm not here to trade barbs with you."

"That's right you had something you wished to discuss." He swallowed the contents of his drink. The longer she was in his home the harder it was becoming to keep his hands to himself. Perhaps drinking was a foolish idea, but it kept him busy on something other than her. He filled his glass once again and turned his attention to her. "What are you waiting for? Tell me why I'm honored with your presence after I don't know how many years."

"Fifteen," she replied.

"Heh?"

"It has been, well almost, fifteen years since you left for Eton. You didn't write, you never came home again, and you forgot about me." She played with her skirt. "The anniversary of the end of our friendship is in less than a sennight, but I don't expect you to remember."

"Right again," he said. The truth would be his to own. Maybe one day he'd explain it all. Today wasn't that day. "But we've digressed again. Please state your reason for coming here today. I'd like to retire for the evening and this conversation has grown tedious."

"It's simple really," Juliette said. "I need you to marry me."

"Come again?" He had to have heard her wrong. How much of the brandy had he imbibed?

"You promised me," she explained. "If I ever needed you, you'd be there for me." She lifted her lashes and stared into his eyes. "My life depends on your willingness to assist me. This is imperative, please say you'll help me."

Bloody hell... How could he say no to that?

Easy enough, open up his mouth and utter the words she didn't want to hear. "No."

The Duke of Kissinger wasn't the marrying sort and it was better she understood that straight away.

CHAPTER 3

"No?" The blasted man had dismissed her without hearing her out. "That's it? You won't even listen to me?"

"If it is to beg me to marry you," he replied. "Then we're done. There's nothing more to say on the matter."

Ohhhh. He was so obstinate. She wanted to shake him and make him see reason. Unfortunately that wouldn't garner in any good. Juliette didn't believe in wasting her time. He'd left her no choice but to make him listen. Nothing would make her move from his home until he did. The dastardly duke owed her at least that much.

"I understand." She forced herself to continue meeting his gaze. "I'd hope the rumors weren't true."

"Trust me they're much worse," he replied in a husky tone. "Maybe one day I'll share some of my more titillating stories with you."

"Oh?" Juliette lifted a brow. As if she wanted to hear about him with other women, but perhaps that was the point. He hoped to scare her into silence. She'd bet every last bit of her pin money he'd not appreciate it being turned back on him. "What's stopping you? I'd love to hear some of your seedier tales. It's past time we reacquainted ourselves with each other." She patted the settee, batting her eyelashes at him. "Come sit down and tell me everything."

"You're an unnatural female," he blustered. "Leave it to you to take the fun out of everything."

Well that went better than she'd anticipated. He'd not be unloading his more lecherous proclivities upon her. Juliette was grateful as she'd not been particularly keen about listening to any of it.

"Are you ready to pay attention now?" She sipped on her brandy. Her life depended on him agreeing to marry her. "I'm rather tired. It's been a trying day. I'd like to settle this so we can move onto the next step."

"There is no next step," Grayson replied. "I believe I said no."

Juliette would not be deterred. Her whole life everything good had either been taken away or put on hold. At one time this man before her had been on the list of good things. She'd like for him to be on that list once again. Either way it didn't change her current situation. Without Grayson's help she'd be left with little choice. Marrying Lord Payne wasn't something she could stomach, and might not live through if even a fraction of what she'd heard was true. Most people didn't pay her any mind and she'd overheard details not meant for innocent ears.

"My father has arranged a marriage for me..."

"Good then you don't need me." He turned away from her. "Glad we had this chat."

What would it take to make him understand how dire her situation was? He'd understand once she said the name of the man her father intended to betroth her to. If she'd heard about his sadistic demeanor, then Grayson would probably have first-hand knowledge. Juliette took a deep breath and said, "Lord Payne."

Grayson whipped around and met her gaze. "Viscount Payne?"

"Is there any other Lord Payne you're familiar with?"

He shook his head and narrowed his eyes. "What does the lord in question have to do with anything?"

"Not much," she said in feigned nonchalance. "He's only my intended groom."

A string of curse words came out of his mouth that should have made Juliette blush. Finally he was beginning to understand the dire nature of her situation. Maybe she should have led with that information. It might have saved her some time. As stubborn as Grayson was though, she doubted it.

"He's to sign the contract within the sennight." She stood and walked over to him. "Less than that from what my father told me earlier. I can't marry him. I'd prefer to stay a spinster living in a cozy cottage with a bunch of cats for company. Anything is preferable to marrying that dreadful man." She nibbled on her bottom lip. "I'm desperate or I wouldn't be here. I'd hoped you would recall the long ago promise and honor it. Please, Gray, help me. If you marry me I'll have the protection of your name. There would be nothing my father or Lord Payne could do."

He scrubbed his hands over his face and sighed. "I don't want to marry. It's nothing to do with you, in fact, you deserve far better than the likes of me." His eyes were filled with a misery she didn't understand.

The joking rake had disappeared and a piece of the Grayson she'd used to know stood before her. "I did make you a promise, and I should keep it. You're right, Lord Payne can't have you."

"You won't regret helping me."

"I already do." He cupped her cheek in his hand. "I'll marry you even though everything inside of me says it's a terrible idea."

She didn't understand why he thought it would be that bad. What reason could he possibly have for believing that. Surely he'd want an heir of his own. A tingle spread through her at the idea of lying with him. He was a renowned rake and ladies sought him out as a lover. It wouldn't be all bad—it couldn't be.

"I understand," she replied.

"Good." He said. "Then you'll also understand it will be a marriage in name only. It's all you need, and as a duchess no one will question you."

There went her dreams of having his children. Maybe in time he'd change his mind. For now it was a victory for him to agree to the marriage. "If that's what you want," she agreed. "I'm grateful you're willing to help."

"Good," he said. "Make yourself comfortable it's going to be a long ride to Gretna Green and I have arrangements to make."

Her mouth opened with shock. "You want us to leave immediately?"

The situation was dire, but did it necessitate they head toward Scotland immediately? He was right in that it was a long journey. A four days ride at the very least, but it would probably be much longer than that in truth. They'd have to stop along the way and change horses. That alone would delay the trips progress, and it didn't take into account any stops for food or other necessities.

"You're here, and at some point your family will realize you're gone." He sighed. "If you want to see this wedding through we need to make sure they don't figure out where or what you have planned and prevent it. I may be a duke, but no respectable family wants to tie me to theirs."

"You're right."

"Say that again." His lips tilted upward. "I may never hear those words from you again."

Her lips twitched at his light teasing. He wasn't brooding any longer and it was a preferable state. She hated seeing him so melancholy. Even his roguish teasing was better than that. They might have a chance of connecting once again. Juliette hoped they would be able to. The walls he'd erected were high and sturdy, but if she was determined enough, and Juliette believed she was, she could knock them down.

"Didn't you have some plans to make?"

"Indeed I did," he replied. "Wait here and when everything is ready I'll retrieve you so we can depart." With that pronouncement he spun on his heels and exited the room.

GRAYSON HEADED up to his room and shut the door. He leaned his head against it and knocked it lightly against the sturdy wood. What the hell happened downstairs? Was he really going to marry Lady Juliette Brooks. His friends would laugh hysterically when they received word of his downfall. They'd not understand the *whys* of it. Hell, he wasn't even sure he wanted to explain it to them. Not once since he'd made their acquaintance had he mentioned his friendship with Juliet. He'd done everything in his power to put her in the past and keep her there.

What kind of husband could he possibly be? He had no idea how to act decent any more. He'd embraced the life of debauchery and hadn't seen any reason to stop. For her he'd have to make an effort. If he continued on the path he was on she'd become a laughing stock in society. She was his first friend and he respected her too much to put her through any of that.

Grayson had told her he had to make plans for their departure. That in itself was a lie. His staff would take care of everything all he had to do was give the order. He'd actually needed time away from her to think. After they were married she'd be his. Why had he told her the marriage would be in name only? What cruel joke was he playing on himself? The only way he'd be able to hold to that was to live in a different house than her. Just being in the same room as her made him itch to touch her. Her skin was creamy and he wanted to find out if it was as soft as it appeared. Juliette's kid skin gloves beckoned to him. At the first opportunity he wanted to unbutton them, peel them off, and kiss the palm of her hand. There were so many things he craved to do to her, with her, he'd lost count of them all. She'd always fascinated him, but now it was on an entirely different level.

A knock on the door brought him back to the present. He'd escaped Juliette's company to make plans for their departure, and he'd yet to make any.

"Pardon me, Your Grace," Burrows called

through the door. "I'm wondering what you'd like for me to do with Lady Juliette."

So did he. Damned if he had any idea. He took a deep breath and opened the door. "Burrows I'm glad you sought me out. Send Smythe upstairs. I need him to prepare my trunk for travel. Also have a footman ready my carriage. Lady Juliette and I are leaving immediately."

"As you wish, Your Grace." Burrows nodded and turned to leave.

It gave Grayson a few more moments to be alone. Soon Smythe, his valet, would arrive and he'd not have any peace for many days. The journey to Scotland would be tiresome and not leave them much privacy. He prayed her father wouldn't guess Juliette had come to him, and definitely not uncover their plans for elopement. There shouldn't be any reason for him to come to that conclusion. Over the years he had made sure to be careful where Juliette was concerned. She might not realize it but everything he did had been for her. His father had threatened her family, and he still had no idea why. What did he gain from keeping them apart? Grayson hadn't become the obedient boy he'd hoped for, and he sure as hell hadn't bowed down to him when he reached his majority. The only favor he'd done for Grayson was dying a few years ago. He'd finally been freed from his control once and for all.

"You summoned me, Your Grace," Smythe said.

"Yes," Grayson turned to him. "Pack my trunk and see it loaded on my carriage. Have a maid pack some of my mother's gowns she left in residence. They're going to be needed for Lady Juliette." They would be a little long, but should fit her otherwise. His mother hadn't stayed in the ducal townhouse since his father died so they were outdated fashions, but they'd work until he could hire a seamstress to make her more.

"I'll make sure it's all done. Is there anything else you require of me?"

"No. That's all."

Smythe bowed and started on the task Grayson gave him. There was one task he had to take care of himself. He went over to the lock box in his room and opened it. Inside, nestled on blue velvet, was his mother's betrothal ring. She'd given it to him upon his father's passing and told him to start searching for his own duchess. He'd ignored her demand and had no intention of using the ring. If given time he'd have purchased a new one for his intended.

Maybe he still would, but for the moment his mother's would do. She'd deserved a ring as a token of his commitment. He'd give it to her on the journey. At least the sapphires would sort of match her eyes—although he doubted a gem could even come close to their sea-green depths.

After a period of time passed giving the servants to prepare the carriage, Burrows came to inform him everything was ready for their departure. "Thank you Burrows. I'll inform Lady Juliette myself."

He left his room leaving his temporary sanctuary behind. Juliette was where he'd left her, lounging on the settee. "Are you ready?"

"Nothing I'd rather do than travel to Scotland with you." She flashed him a warm smile. "Lead the way, Your Grace."

Grayson bit back a retort. Juliette had never been formal with him and he found he didn't like it. Whatever her reason was for doing so now he'd figure it out later. They had more important things to do. Besides they had a long journey ahead and a lot of time to play the question game. He'd figure out what was going on inside that pretty head of hers before they reached their destination.

Grayson helped Juliette into the carriage, then joined her inside. He took the seat across from her afraid to be too close to her warmth. It was going to be a very long sennight at this rate.

"Don't worry no one is going to stop us."

He wasn't entirely sure if that was a good thing or not. "Trust me. I'm not giving it a second thought." Grayson stared out the window at the night sky. It wasn't as clear in London as it was at his childhood home, but it gave him something to concentrate on. "Make yourself comfortable. Rest if you're able to. It will be a while before we stop to exchange horses."

Grayson leaned his head against the back of the coach and feigned sleep. It would give him some measure of comfort, and maybe she'd take her cue from him to rest.

CHAPTER 4

Juliette stared across the carriage and attempted to make out Grayson's features in the dark. The shadow that marked the spot on his seat hadn't moved or made a sound in what seemed like forever. How could he sleep? It was near impossible for her to find any comfort, let alone rest, between the rocking carriage and frigid weather.

"Gray," she called out to him. No answer, blasted man—she didn't believe he was sleeping. Why was he pretending? Was it so tedious to converse with her? "Your Grace," Juliette said, "I've been thinking..." Maybe if she started talking she'd force him to acknowledge he was very much awake. The more outlandish the statement, the more likely he'd be unable to resist responding. "After we're married, I'll travel to Rome. You don't want a wife around hindering your—proclivities—and I've always wanted to visit Italy. Your comment about lions earlier brought it to mind."

Still nothing from his side of the carriage. She might have to bring it up a notch—or twelve. Good thing she was more than up to the challenge. "I've read a lot about the Colosseum and the gladiator matches." Juliette paused hoping he'd interrupt, but when he didn't she continued, "Venatores and Bestiarii were a special class of warrior that tangled with a variety of wild beasts. It was more of a gruesome animal hunt, not unlike a hunt sponsored by one of our lords happy to bring an innocent beastie to ground. Lions were a favored species on these hunts. They weren't the main show—the gladiators were there for that, but they did open the festivities and help feed the blood lust or the spectators. Of course the poor things weren't always slaughtered for sport, they were also used for executions."

"Is there a point to all this drivel?"

"Yes, I wanted to explain my interest in Rome and why I'll take a trip there after the wedding." Her lips tilted upward. Blasted man couldn't stop himself from responding. "Since it will be a marriage in name only I don't see why I should stay and run your household. I trust you have competent staff to see to all of it."

"You're not going to Rome by yourself, brat."

Oh how she wished she could see his face. It was so hard to gauge his reaction without properly seeing his features. "Oh?" She raised an eyebrow. "Did you want to go too? I didn't think touring the ruins would be to your taste."

"No I have no desire to go to bloody Rome, or any place far from the comfort of my own bed. Let me rephrase that for you—I'm not going to allow you to go anywhere other than to my townhouse or my country estate. I can't very well protect you if you're constantly putting yourself in danger." He sighed and the shadow like shape across from her moved.

She considered his words and how best to respond. As children they used to talk for hours on all the things they found fascinating. To her this was no different. Rome and the Colosseum had been interesting to her, especially since her social interactions had been limited. It gave her a reason to escape her mundane life and visit exotic locales through the pages of a book. Truthfully it had been enough for her to read about them, but since he was forbidding her... Well, she'd have to protest. He'd left her little choice on the matter.

"I never took you for a spoil sport," she responded. "With the reputation you've cultivated over the years, one would think you were all for anything considered risky or adventurous."

Every time she came across his name in the scandal sheet a piece of her heart died. She didn't know why he'd taken the path he'd chosen, but it was far from the boy she'd called a friend. A part of her believed he'd done it to distance himself from the pain in his life. His father hadn't been a kind man, and the little she interacted with him gave her a bad impression of his demeanor. Her own father wasn't a great man and made choices she abhorred—her betrothal a case in point, but she believed he loved her in his own way. The previous duke didn't appear to have a warm spot in his whole body. He was cold and unforgiving.

Juliette believed the only reason her family socialized with Grayson's was because her mother was fast friends with the duchess. Her father and Gray's had little in common. The duke was very active in parliament, and her father barely kept up with any of it. The earl loved hunting and the duke thought it was tedious and scoffed at the idea. They were as opposite as two individuals could be, but somehow they'd always come together at Christmastide.

"And what do you know of my reputation?" He chuckled "You hinted at the rumors before, and I believe I mentioned they're much worse. Do you want me to share now?"

She didn't really and he probably knew it too, but she'd brought it up. Trust Grayson to run with what he believed would make her uncomfortable. "If you're in the mood to tell tales by all means begin. Why don't we start with the day you left to Eton. I'd so hate to miss any part of what you've been doing since we last spoke."

"Ah Jules," he said warmly. "I do believe I'm going to enjoy reacquainting myself with you."

"So does that mean we're sharing life stories?" She asked. "or are we pretending the years of your silence never existed."

It pained her to admit how much his abandonment hurt her—a betrayal she'd not quite recovered from. If she'd had another choice, she'd not have gone to him for aid. Her father and evil step-mother, were the reason she sat on the other side of the carriage. In some ways she wanted to thank them for pushing her to seek Grayson out. She'd always wanted to ask him why he'd left without saying good bye. There was so much she didn't understand and believed she'd been owed an explanation. Now that they were to be married perhaps she'd finally have the answers she desired.

"Those years won't go away. They're solidly a part of who we are now," he said gravely. "As much as I'd like to will them away it's an impossible feat. As to sharing our stories..." He paused a moment and took a deep breath. "I'd rather avoid that as well. A lot of my past is best left where it is—behind me. Looking back won't change a damn thing. We will go from this point on, and hope the fates are kind enough to make us both find some measure of happiness."

It was a pretty speech, but Juliette didn't like one word he'd said. He wanted to brush everything under the rug and expected her to accept it. Why? Because he'd made a pronouncement and his word was law. She suppressed an unladylike snort, and replied, "That's a fascinating bit of nonsense. Your past is a part of you and what made you into this insufferable cad before me. I'd like to one day understand it, but I won't force it on you." She grinned wickedly. If he could see her he'd have run fast in the other direction. It was time to poke the beast. "Since you're forbidding me to visit Rome and see the

Colosseum in person…" She sighed whimsically. "I had so hoped to have the opportunity to picture those strong viral beasts fighting battle after battle. It must have been amazing."

"The lions would appreciate your passion for their skills in battle," he replied dryly. "But I must insist you stay in England."

"Oh I wasn't talking about the lions, but don't misunderstand me. I do find them fascinating." She fanned herself. "The gladiators though—they must have been so skilled and brave. Some of them might have been handsome, but all of them surely were as brawn and manly as a male could be. My imagination has been running wild on what they could've looked like. Do you have any ideas?"

"Why the bloody hell would I imagine what another male would look like?" He growled. "And neither should you."

It took everything inside of her not to laugh hysterically. This was so much fun. The trip to Scotland had just become infinitely better. He'd be so entertaining if it was this easy to provoke him. "Why ever not? What good is an imagination if you can't use it properly?"

"It's rather, well, ladies don't picture men or what their supposed appearances. It's not done."

Juliette snorted. It couldn't be helped. Now he was being ridiculous. "It's hypocritical of you to chastise me for merely envisioning a man in any form when your reputation suggests you've enjoyed females in ways my imagination hasn't breached."

"One doesn't have anything to do with the other," he replied. "It might not be fair, but females are held to a higher standard."

Statements such as that one wouldn't endear him to her. She should kick him for good measure. Males were so obstinate, and Grayson topped the list of stubborn fools more than any other. Once upon a time she'd thought the sun rose and set on him. He'd been her everything, and now she wondered who he really was. Sadly though, he was right. Society expected women to remain innocent and learn next to nothing about the world. Many men, and women alike, would be scandalized to realize she'd read about Rome, the Colosseum, and gladiators. Education was to be kept to mundane things such as watercolors, sewing, and music lessons. A well accomplished lady had proper deportment and decorum at all times.

"Lucky for you," she replied. "Your wife won't be as boring as to follow the rules set by society. I plan on keeping you guessing for the rest of your life."

A truer statement had never been uttered. She didn't like to be predictable, and hiding in dark corners had never appealed to her. It had become necessary when Eloise had entered her life. Escaping the countess's notice had grown into a game of sorts. If she didn't cross her path Eloise almost forgot she existed. For a time it had worked, until her little brother was born and her step-mother saw Juliette as competition for the earl's affection. She fully believed that was why Eloise was pushing her father to tie Juliette to Lord Payne in marriage. Now that she was on the brink of being free from her family she refused to hide herself ever again.

"My dear, none of that surprises me. You've been shocking me since the moment you entered my home. Why would I expect anything less?"

She smiled. "At least one of us had been predictable in a sense."

"What's that supposed to mean?" he asked affronted.

"I expected a rake," she replied. "You put on a good show at first, but I have to say I'm rather disappointed. You're rather—tame."

If that didn't result in a rise of outrage nothing would. Was it too much to desire a kiss from her intended. All right, he never planned on marrying anyone, outright refused her, and of course never asked for her hand, but he *was* going to marry her despite all of that. Juliette had never been kissed and more than anything she wanted him to be the one to do it.

"Are you challenging me?"

She shrugged, but wasn't sure if he could see the gesture. "Of course not. It was an observation. If you're the scoundrel everyone claims you to be wouldn't you have already taken advantage of the situation? No one is stopping you, and we do intend to marry at the end of this journey."

"I'm not a seducer of innocents," he proclaimed. "And I'll be damned if I start with you."

Juliette sighed. *Drat.* Grayson was going to be difficult, and she wasn't entirely sure how to achieve her goal. An idea formed in her mind and before she changed her mind she said, "I suppose I'll have to have an affair. Otherwise I'll never know true passion..."

Juliette sat back and waited for his response. It was bound to be good.

CHAPTER 5

"By all means, do." There wasn't a chance in hell he'd allow her to find a lover. If another man so much as looked at her wrong he'd rip him to shreds. Grayson clenched his fists and kept his anger, and yes, jealousy, in check. If he exploded now she'd realize how much her statement bothered him. He couldn't have that. She'd already owned far more of him than he was comfortable admitting. So his words belied what he truly felt. "I have no plans of ceasing any of my more pleasurable pursuits."

"That's generous of you," she replied. "You're not worried about being cuckolded?"

"My dear," he said with sincerity. "A man is only a cuckold if he's unaware or cares about his wife's dalliances." The sun was beginning to rise in the sky and her face was becoming more visible. Like a cloud moving away from the sun she was a bright beacon that brought warmth to his weary soul. "All I ask is you're—discreet."

It was becoming harder and harder to hold back his true feelings. He hated the idea of her with another man, always had. But as long as he'd kept a distance her potential lover or husband was ignorable. With her present, and oh so close, the possibility of it ate at him. How could he expect her to remain chaste, especially as he refused to touch her. He had to reassess his earlier proclamation. The only way he'd be able to avoid caressing her was to avoid her all together, and yet even that didn't sit well with him.

"This is rather enlightening." Her lips tilted upward. "So far I'd have to say the only downfall marriage to you would bring is your insistence I remain in England. I'll take that as a challenge." She waved her hand. "After a while you'll gladly send me packing."

He gritted his teeth. She could do her worst, but she'd not leave England without his protection. There were things in the world she didn't understand or couldn't be learned from a book. Juliette was innocent and couldn't comprehend the depravity seeping into the world. Grayson would ensure she didn't ever experience the seedier part of society. When she sought his protection of his name she'd unwittingly agreed to his need to shield her as he saw fit. In time she'd realize he only had her best interests in mind when he dictated his demands.

"Not bloody likely," he replied. "Nothing you could do or say would make me budge on that particular detail."

"We'll see," she replied. "It feels as if we've been in this carriage forever. When do you think we'll stop?"

Not soon enough in his estimation. Time away from her, and a moment to stretch his legs, were both very much needed. Sadly, he'd not have either one of them for several more hours. He'd ordered his driver to take a median pace. There was no need to rush and run the horses to ground, but he still wanted to arrive in Scotland as soon as possible.

"We will stop in the first town we reach around the midday meal. If you're hungry cook packed a few provisions for the journey."

"No," she said. "I'm too nervous to eat." Juliette

rubbed her hands together and blew on them. "It's just... I'm cold. The blanket isn't enough."

Grayson sighed. He should be a gentleman and offer her his blanket, but he was cold too. The best solution to both of their problems was to offer to double up the blankets and share body heat. But that would mean he'd be in even closer proximity to her. If he held her in his arms he wouldn't be responsible for his actions. His hands would wander over her lush frame and he'd take full advantage of her. It was wrong, but it was who he was. She was to be his wife —didn't he have the right to stroke her any way he chose? Thoughts such as that one would surely lead to nowhere but trouble.

"Join me over here and bring your blanket," he said, resigned. He couldn't allow her to freeze. What kind of cad would allow a lady to shiver when there was an acceptable answer to the problem? One who was afraid of what the lady's closeness meant to his reputation. Grayson was supposed to be a rake—a scoundrel comfortable with debauchery, and he was felled by a mere lady. "I'll keep you warm."

Juliette didn't hesitate at his suggestion. He'd give her that much... Her bravery put the most hardened soldier to shame. Grayson lifted his blanket and she sat next to him, and handed her blanket to him. In one quick motion he had it spread over top of them both. With the double thickness of two blankets and their body heat spread over him.

"You're so warm," Juliette said and cuddled into him. She wrapped her arms around his waist and laid her head on his chest. "Why didn't we do this sooner?"

Because he was an inconsiderate arse. "Did you manage any sleep?"

"No," she shook her head. "I was cold and uncomfortable." Her mouth opened wide as a yawn overtook her. "Though now that I have you as a cushion it might be possible."

Juliette wiggled and nestled more firmly against him. His entire body tightened with each move she made. His need heightened to a painful state. She was going to kill him. "Try and sleep. We have hours before we stop again."

"I might," she replied. "Gray?"

What would it take for her to stop moving, talking, or damn well driving him mad? "Are you going to ramble incessantly the entire time we're on the road to Scotland?"

She was quiet for several heartbeats. He'd started

to believe she finally closed her eyes and went to sleep, but she'd had something else in mind. The more time he spent in her company the more he believed she'd be the death of him.

"I know you said our marriage would be in name only, and you don't mind if I find a lover, but..."

He closed his eyes and prayed for patience. What was she up to now? "Do you need me to say it again?" God help him, but he didn't know if he could give her what she wanted. His desire for her was increasing at an alarming rate.

"No. I understood the first time." She tilted her head and met his gaze. Her hand slid lower and rested at the edge of his trousers. His breath froze in his lungs. "What must I do to convince you I'd prefer you be my first—everything."

Grayson had been right, having her sit next to him was a bad idea. Her brazen touch was undoing his already weakened resolve. He couldn't fight her and himself—it was a futile effort. Somehow he had to rein in them both, and he had no idea how to halt it. "I'm honored..." The words he'd intended to say somehow had become lodged in his throat. Hurting her had always sat wrong with him. If he continued he'd crush her, and he couldn't do that. Nonchalance was one thing, but out and out cruelty he'd hoped to avoid.

"Don't say any more," she said after a moment. "I realized a long time ago I was no great beauty. My step-mother has told me on more than one occasion at best I can be described as plain. I won't push you to be with me if you're having trouble finding even an inkling of desire to do so."

Plain? He was baffled she believed she was unremarkable. She'd mentioned being a wallflower, but even that still confounded him. The part of him that always found her lovely, and always would, wanted to protest on her behalf. If she realized how crazy he was to touch her she'd never let this idea of hers go. There would be no going back if he gave in to the craving he carried inside of him.

"It isn't that..."

"You don't need to explain," she said sadly. "I understand."

She didn't though, not at all. If she did she'd have an entirely different attitude toward him. Grayson didn't deserve her or what she offered. He was tainted by his choices. At the time he believed he was making the right decision. His father had put strict dictates in place and Gray had been expected to follow them to the letter. After he'd been forced to sever his friendship with her he'd lost all reason and went to the dark side of his nature. Once he embraced every depravity he could he realized there was no going back. He could never resume their friendship, and she'd be far better without him in her life.

"Jules," he said reassuringly. "You're not plain. Don't let anyone ever convince you of that claptrap ever again."

He couldn't agree to be her lover, but he could convince her she was beautiful. It wouldn't be a hardship or a lie. She was gorgeous inside and out. Her step-mother was probably jealous of her and set out to make Juliette doubt her own worth. Women let their claws out at the first sign of competition, and Jules was indeed that in the Riverdale household. It was a shame the earl hadn't married a kinder woman. Juliette's mother had been one of the most gracious and thoughtful women he'd known. Which was more than he could say for his own mother—she'd abandoned him at the first sign of adversity, maybe if she'd stood up to father his life would have taken a different turn. He'd never know one way or the other. There was no room for regrets in his life. He fully believed the past was left where it was, quite firmly behind him.

"You're only being nice because you think my feelings are hurt." She laid her head down on his chest once again. "Don't worry about me. I'm all right with being forgettable. In a way it makes things easier. When no one sees you they say some very interesting things. I've overheard a lot of titillating information by being invisible."

That had to be the saddest thing he'd ever heard in his life. "There is nothing good about going unnoticed. What kind of fools have you been socializing with?"

"Socializing is too strong a word for what I've been allowed to do." She sighed. "First I was in mourning, and then father remarried." Juliet raised her hand higher up his stomach leaving a trail of pleasure that continued on as she drew circles on his chest with her forefinger. He could become accustomed to her touch rather easily. "After that he forgot I existed until Eloise decided I must marry and leave my father's care. At first it sounded wonderful. My first season had been cut short, and I did long to have my own family. Now I'd rather have the freedom to choose for myself my own destiny."

"If you didn't go out in society" —he paused and took a deep breath— "How did you overhear anything at all?" He'd not realized she'd been secluded from society? His informants failed to tell him she'd not returned to *ton* after her mourning period. But to be fair all he ever asked is if she was happy and healthy. It had been enough to know she was alive and well. The rest would have been a torture he'd not have been able to endure.

"My father had occasional dinner parties, and I was allowed to attend them." She continued to run her fingers over his chest. He never wanted her to stop. "And sometimes he'd have a visitor. No one paid me any mind."

They were all fools, especially her father. Grayson could take comfort in knowing she'd never endure indifference from him again. No, she'd endure it from him. How was he any better than what she'd been living with. He didn't like the conclusion he was drawing from himself to her father.

"As a duchess you'll be able to command society and set trends," he said. It was all he could bring himself to offer.

"I never wanted to be sought after by the *ton*," she said quietly. "All I ever wanted was to be loved by one person completely."

His heart beat rapidly in his chest. He wanted to hug her tight against him and reassure her he'd love her always, but wouldn't make a promise he couldn't keep. Lucky, or maybe unlucky, for him he was saved from responding. The carriage rocked as it hit a jut in the road and wobbled back and forth. Then a crack echoed on the wind as they crashed on the side of the road.

CHAPTER 6

S tabbing pain shot through Juliette's head. She lifted her hand and placed it over the throbbing ache. What happened? The last thing she recalled was—had Grayson been about to say something? Damn it was all fuzzy inside her head. She rolled to her side and searched for him. He'd been by her side, and keeping her warm, now she was cold and alone.

"Gray?" she mumbled.

Juliette scrambled to her feet, her heart raced inside her chest. The carriage was slightly tilted and the door swung open. Wind whistled through the carriage and sending goose bumps up her arm. The biting cold settled deep inside her and if she didn't do something soon she'd freeze. Where was

Grayson? Carefully she slid out of the carriage and stepped warily onto solid ground. She scanned the area searching for him. Not too far away from the entrance to the carriage she found him sprawled on the ground.

His eyes were closed and blood dripped from a gash on his forehead. She knelt beside him and cupped his face in her hands. "Grayson." Her voice wavered with barely restrained emotion. She brushed her fingers through his hair and said, "Please open your eyes."

He had to be all right. She refused to accept anything less. It was her fault they were on the road to Scotland. If she'd not insisted they marry he'd be safe at home. Juliette stood and scanned the area. The driver was a few feet ahead sitting on the ground. She rushed to his side and helped him to his feet. "His Grace is injured. I need your help with him."

He looked past her and cursed. "We hit a rut in the road and it threw a wheel. We're still a mile outside the nearest village. I'll have to ride one of the horses for help."

Juliette glanced from Grayson and then back to the driver. It would be up to her to see to Grayson's care while the driver went for help. The wind was too strong and biting to stay outside the carriage, but tilted as it was they couldn't sit inside of it either. They couldn't stay in the cold for too long... "Please hurry. I'll grab the blankets from the carriage and keep him as warm as possible until you return."

"I'll be back before you realize I'm gone," he promised.

The driver unhitched a horse, hopped on its back, and headed toward the nearby town. Juliette prayed he'd return fast. She turned to the carriage and grabbed the blankets. Grayson needed to be kept warm, but she didn't have a clue how to ensure it. The ground was hard and cold. It wouldn't provide any of the necessary warmth even with the blankets on top of him. When she'd cuddled with him in the carriage it had helped. Perhaps that was the solution to her problem. If she were to wrap herself over him along with the blankets she'd be able to aide in keeping the cold at bay.

She spread one blanket over top of him, and then the other over it. Then studied her handiwork. He seemed rather uncomfortable, but it was hard to tell. Maybe something to cushion his head would help. She went back to the carriage and grabbed her hand muff. It was small, but large enough for a pillow to cushion his head. Carefully she lifted his head and placed it underneath. Satisfied with the result, she crawled under the blanket with him and wrapped her arms around his torso.

The ground was colder than Juliette realized and she shivered involuntarily. She laid her head on his chest and prayed they'd be rescued soon. After several moments warmth began to spread over her. It wasn't much, but enough to make the cold more bearable.

"Don't worry, Gray," she said. It was more for herself than him. He was unconscious and unlikely to reply. "The driver will be back before we know it. Then we can take sanctuary in a nice warm inn while they fix the wheel. I'm so sorry, more than I can say. This is all my fault."

It wasn't too late to rectify any of it. After she saw him safe and sound in the inn she'd turn back. Marriage to Lord Payne would be awful, but at least she would know Grayson was safe. In the end that was all that mattered to her. He might have complained, and on the outset said no, but he'd come through for her. When she decided to ask for his help she knew he'd not turn her away. There was some of the boy she'd grown up with still in the man —however faint it was.

She lifted her head and memorized his features. The boy had been soft and more pretty than handsome. The man was breathtaking. The soft edges had formed into high cheekbones, and soft full—kissable lips. He'd refused to kiss her. Juliette craved his lips on hers more than she'd ever wanted anything. One kiss and maybe then she could go on with life, satisfied.

What if she never got the chance. Should she take it now? Would he be upset if she did? She bit her lip and considered. It would be wrong to do something against his will, but she couldn't resist kissing him. It wasn't a kiss the way she wanted, but one of comfort. She leaned down and pressed her lips to his forehead. "I'll be by your side as long as you need me." Then she laid her head on his chest and snuggled against him.

That is the way she stayed until the driver returned with help. After they had Grayson loaded in the carriage they all headed back toward the village. The innkeeper and a couple of brawny lads helped carry him up to a room they'd prepared. A doctor had been summoned. Juliette sat in the main room and waited for the prognosis. As soon as they let her she'd return to his side. He was her responsibility and she'd make sure he made a full recovery.

SOMEONE WAS BEATING his head with a hammer. Whoever dared was going to feel the back of his fist in their face. Grayson slowly opened his eyes and found the soft glow of candlelight. Juliet sat in a chair next to the bed. Her head lulled back against the chair. Her dark tresses were unbound and falling over her shoulder. He wanted to reach over and stoke them. They looked so soft inviting—hell everything about her did. Where were they? The last thing he remembered was being in the carriage, and then... Had they been in an accident?

He stretched his arms and fell back on the bed once again. The sharp pain shooting through his head was agonizing. Grayson lifted his hands and rubbed his temples. The torment dulled to a mild, and tolerable ache.

"You're awake," she said.

Slowly he turned to meet her gaze. "What happened?"

"Carriage wheel broke. It will be prepared by morning."

That explained part of it, but he still didn't understand how he ended up in a warm bed with her keeping vigil. "How long have I been out?"

"Not too long," she replied. "Well most of the day. You missed the midday meal. The doctor doesn't want you to have anything heavy. So the cook is making you a nice broth. It should arrive shortly if you're hungry."

His stomach rumbled at the mention of food. "I don't care what the doctor said. Broth won't be enough. Have them bring me a full meal."

Grayson realized he sounded like a petulant child, but his head hurt and he was hungry. The Duke of Kissinger always got what he wanted, and he wanted food, darn it. He turned his head a little too fast and the pain returned in full force. A wince escaped him before he could stop it.

"You're being absurd," she chastised. "Here let me massage your head. Just close your eyes and relax."

Juliette sat down on the bed next to him and placed her hands on either side of his head. She pressed her delicate fingers against his temples and rubbed slowly. He moaned in pleasure. The pain disappeared under her careful ministrations. It was amazing and he'd gladly lay there forever if she allowed it.

A knock echoed through the room and firmly ending the pleasure she'd been administering. She stood quickly and went to see who disturbed their peace. Juliette opened the door and greeted the interloper. Grayson wanted them gone so she could return to attending him. When she returned to his side she carried a tray with two mugs. Steam rose out of each one and his stomach rumbled again at the scents wafting from them.

"What is that?"

"These," she gestured toward them. "Are the broth you didn't want. Do you wish for me to send them back down to the kitchen?"

Was she only having broth too? She should have more sustenance. There was no reason for her to abstain—she'd not been injured or had she? "Give me a mug. You should go down to the kitchen and eat something. Broth isn't enough for you."

Juliette shook her head. "Both are for you." She set the tray on the chair and turned to him. "Let me help you sit up."

She thought she was going to take care of him? In a way he supposed she had been. But now that he was awake he'd not let her cater to his every need. The pain was already easing in his head and he could damn well sit up on his own. "I can do it myself." He struggled to a sitting position and then turned toward her. Grayson flashed her a smug smile. "Hand me a mug."

Juliette picked one up and gave it to him. He took a slow sip and let the flavor settle on his tongue. It tasted so damn good he sighed in delight. It was a nice beef broth with a hint of onion and sage. She'd said both were for him. If that was true when would she find sustenance? "Have you eaten?"

"Don't worry about me," she said. "I've had plenty to eat."

He sipped more broth and stared at her over the rim of the mug. "What are you not telling me?" She was acting rather evasive.

"Nothing," she replied a little too fast.

Grayson narrowed his gaze and said, "I'm not a dimwitt. Tell me now."

Juliette fidgeted a moment and then moved toward the chair. She picked up the tray and set it on the bed beside him. Grayson downed the contents of the mug in his hand and set it on the tray. He picked the other one up and took a drink. He waited patiently, or as much as he was able to, for her to speak. She had a confession, or an idiotic notion, and it would take her a moment or two to divulge it. As a child she'd done something similar. It was rather nice to see some things didn't change.

"It hasn't escaped me that you'd not have been hurt if not for me," she finally said. "If you don't want to go through with the marriage, I understand. In fact, I think we should return to London. Maybe I can try reasoning with my father."

Grayson clenched the mug tightly in his hand. Where did she get these hare-brained ideas from? It wasn't her fault the wheel broke on the carriage. "Did you sabotage the wheel?"

"Of course not." She snorted. "Why would I do that?"

"Then I fail to see how you're to blame for any of this." He took another sip of the broth and waited. She'd have some outlandish reason, and it might prove entertaining—if this whole line of thinking hadn't already angered him beyond reason.

"That still doesn't negate my culpability," she said. "You would be at home, warm in your own bed if I hadn't sought your help." She bit her bottom lip. "You could've died, Gray. If that had happened, I'd never forgive myself."

"I'm fine," he said. "This all could've happened at any moment. Don't bother saying what you planned on spouting off next. We're continuing on to Scotland. You're going to be my wife and you best adapt to the idea. I keep my promises."

"If you're sure," she said. "I still think there's time to go back."

He finished the broth and set the mug aside. "Jules, you must realize there's no turning back. You're thoroughly compromised. Not only were you in my home unchaperoned, but we've been alone in my carriage for hours, and I don't know how long in this room. Accept your fate—you will be mine forever and always."

For the first time since she'd shown up at his home the idea of spending the rest of his life with her by his side—felt right. A weight lifted and he realized he'd been wrong. She'd always been the light in his life. He could be better for her and would be.

"You're right," she agreed.

"How about that." He laughed. "Twice in less than a day you're agreeing with me, or has it been more than that. Keep it up and it will be a habit you're unable to break."

She smiled. "Unlikely, but I do have enough intelligence to realize when I'm wrong."

"Come here, Jules." He patted the bed. "Lay down beside me and rest. In the morning we begin our trip again."

His soon to be duchess didn't argue. She picked up the tray and set it back on the chair, then crawled beside him on the bed. He pulled her into his arms and she nestled against him. Her head rested on his chest, and she fell fast asleep. For a moment, everything seemed right in the world, and Grayson started to believe happy endings were possible.

CHAPTER 7

Their trip to Scotland had started all right, was side-lined slightly by a broken wheel, and then resumed without much ado. They'd been back on the road for several days with non-stop travel. Each day had blended into the next. It was hard to tell where one ended and the other started. Perhaps Grayson should have kept better track, and if he'd have to guess it had been over four days inside the coach with Juliette, but honestly it had stopped mattering to him. The end result would still culminate to one thing—them standing together reciting marriage vows.

They didn't stop at an inn overnight again, but they did take small breaks. The horses were changed on a regular basis, and they stretched their legs, or took care of other needs during the process. After the delay with the wheel Grayson hadn't wanted to stop unless it was essential. Something niggled at the bottom of his stomach. He fully believed if they dallied too much they'd not make it to Gretna Green in time.

Juliette believed her father didn't have any idea where she may have gone, and he might not. He didn't want to take any needless chances. She was going to be his wife. Once he made up his mind there was no turning back. That ridiculousness of a name only marriage wasn't happening either. He'd inform her of that when it mattered—on their wedding night.

"I've never been so tired of staring at the inside of a carriage in my life," Juliet complained. "Surely we must be close to Scotland by now."

He didn't blame her one bit. The journey to Scotland's border was long and tedious, and cold as hell in the middle of the winter months. The further they traveled inland the more frigid it seemed to get too. "It won't be long. We should arrive at Gretna Green by nightfall."

"This isn't how I imagined Christmastide to be," she said quietly. "Not that I've had an enjoyable one in a long time."

The last carefree Christmastide he'd experienced was his final one with her. Sure he'd had fun and gave a good resemblance of reveling in the festivities, but his heart hadn't been in it. None of it had ever compared to his childhood—back when he'd been too young for his father to take notice of them. Sometimes he longed for that ignorance. It had been a much simpler time.

"When was the last time Christmastide was worth remembering for you?" He wondered if it was the same time as his. Probably not, but if so they'd have that in common. Although Grayson hoped it wasn't true. He'd wanted her to go on and have many happy times without him.

"The last one that was perfect was with you," she said. "I did have good ones after that. They weren't the same without you, but my mother did her best to make everything around her bright. She was a good woman."

"You miss her." It was a statement more than a question. Of course she'd miss her mother. The countess had been a wonderful woman. It was more than making things bright as Juliette had put it. She was kind and generous to all around her. "She wouldn't want you to be forlorn. I know it's hard, but try to remember the times you were happiest."

She remained quiet and pensive. "Her death was sudden and I didn't have a chance to say goodbye. One day we were planning which balls to attend, and the next she breathed no more." Juliette fidgeted in the seat next to him. "I'm not sure what happened. We were in the sitting room, her face turned red, and she started to rub her arm. Soon after that, she collapsed."

"It had to be difficult to watch," he said quietly. He wasn't entirely sure how his father died and hadn't cared to ask. His mother had barely managed to reach him in time to inform him of his father's death—not that it had mattered much in the end. Grayson had been summoned to return and attend the farce of a funeral his mother arranged at Kissinger Castle. The man who'd sired him hadn't respected him, and therefore Grayson hadn't seen any reason to attend the ceremony honoring his life. His mother still held that against him. She'd called him an ungrateful wretch, and he couldn't argue with her on that assessment. At the very least he *was* a wretch, and hadn't given a damn. He'd not mourned his father, and sure as hell didn't miss the rotten bastard.

"It was," she said. "But it was years ago. I don't

wish to dwell on it. You're right, she wouldn't want me to be sad."

The carriage rolled to a stop. Grayson peeked out the window to check out their surroundings. They halted in front of an inn. "It appears we've arrived. Come let's see if we can let rooms for the night and then see who can perform the ceremony."

Their discussion had taken a turn neither one of them wished to continue. It was morbid and not generally a topic brought up before pending nuptials. Of course most couples on the brink of marriage weren't as melancholy as they'd been. What kind of marriage would they have at this rate? They barely knew each other, and what they did was a piece of their childhood they were probably better off forgetting. Grayson hadn't believed marriage would suit him. It was part of the reason he'd been so adverse to it. The other was he hadn't cared if the ducal line continued. He came from a long line of mean-spirited males. What if he had a son and he was worse than his father had been. Not that Grayson was much better—he'd taken a different path, but it hadn't exactly been decent and caring.

Grayson stepped out of the carriage and then turned to help Juliette out. She placed her gloved hand in his. It was a trusting gesture one born of familiarity. "I'm exhausted. I think when I'm finally able to lay down and sleep in truth it will be for a whole sennight."

He laughed. "I'll be right next to you. It sounds glorious."

They walked into the inn and were greeted by the owner. "How may I help you?"

"We need two of your best rooms," he demanded.

The man moved around restlessly. "I'm sorry but we're full up. We've only one room available."

Of course there was. By the time he planned on sharing it with Juliet they should be man and wife, but he'd hope to give her some privacy. Especially as he'd not explained how he'd decided to no longer have a marriage in name only. He craved to touch her, make love to her, and make her his in every way possible. Grayson was rather proud of his restraint thus far. He'd been the proper gentleman and hadn't even kissed her. Though he'd give anything to touch his lips to hers.

She touched his arm with her hand. He turned and met her gaze. "One room will be fine," she said reassuringly. "We can make do."

He nodded. "Can you direct us to the local parishioner?"

"You're wanting to wed?" The innkeeper grinned. "It is a common occurrence here. We've plenty Englishman bringing their intendeds to elope. The smithy can perform the ceremony."

"The smithy?" he raised an eyebrow.

"Aye," the innkeeper said. "He's a fine set up for weddings. Has everything a couple needs to make the deed legal."

That was what they needed more than anything. To make sure the wedding was legal and binding. If Juliette's father hoped to challenge the match they had to do everything right. Though as a duke, Grayson had a better chance of winning a battle over the legitimacy of his marriage. His name held power, and it was the only thing he was grateful to his father for. It gave him the means to protect Juliette, and he'd take anything within his grasp to ensure that.

"Please direct us to his location," Grayson replied, "And then inform my servant where he can deliver our trunks." He started to walk away with Juliette's arm tucked under his arm, but then stopped. "Can you have a hot bath set up as well."

"Very well, my lord."

"I'm the Duke of Kissinger," Grayson replied. "If everything meets my requirements you will be well rewarded."

"I will ensure it myself," he bowed. "Your Grace."

Grayson led Juliette out of the inn, intending to head straight to the smithy. The sooner they married, the more relaxed he could be. This whole trip had made him overly anxious. Her safety was up to him. If he failed her he'd never forgive himself.

"Pardon me, Your Grace," his driver said. "There's something you should know."

He stopped and met his driver's gaze. "What is it?"

"While I was inquiring about stabling the carriage and our mounts I overheard something."

The man was wearing his patience thin. At the rate he was delivering his news they'd freeze in place. "Let me escort Juliette to the smithy's place of business, and then you can explain it to me. I don't want her standing in the cold."

He nodded. "Please hurry, it's urgent."

Grayson nodded and headed in the direction of the smithy. "You're shaking."

"It's cold," she replied.

"You're not scared are you?" She'd been brave up until this point. Marriage was an important and life altering step. Was she having second thoughts? He hoped not. They'd both made a decision and they were sticking to it. Soon she'd be his duchess in every way. His body ached to join with hers. "There's no turning back now."

"I'm not afraid," she replied. "It really is cold."

He nodded. The more time he spent in Scotland, albeit only a short distance over the border, he hated it. The frigid weather was enough to freeze his bollocks off. He had to take her word for it that it was the chilly temperature causing her to shake. They stopped at a nearby building, and he knocked on the door. It creaked open slowly. A rather rotund man greeted them merrily. "Are you two seeking to be married?"

"We do," Grayson replied. "Can you assist us?"

"Aye," he replied. "Please come in. My daughter and her husband can act as witnesses." He moved aside to allow them to enter. "My name is Elliot."

"It's a pleasure to make your acquaintance, Elliot," Juliette replied. "Thank you so much for letting us intrude on your evening."

"Think nothing of it lass," he said. "You're not the first to do so, and I expect you won't be the last."

Grayson's impatience was running deep. He wanted this done, along with the conversation with his driver. What had the man believed so damn important to interrupt him on the way to his wedding. He wasn't prone to dramatics so it had to be vital. The sooner the ceremony was over the more relaxed he would be.

"Will this take long?" Grayson asked.

"Not at all," the plump man said. He smiled wide, and then a jolly laugh rippled out of him. His white beard matched his hair almost exactly. He wore dark red trousers and a pearly white shirt. His waist coat matched his trousers, save for some white trim. "Clara, Fergus," he called out. "We've a wedding you need to witness."

A woman with pale blond hair and a stunning countenance entered the room. "Fergus will be back soon. He had to run to the inn with a delivery. Is there anything you need me to do before we begin?"

"Aye, grab me a spot of ribbon from your sewing kit."

"I've found a ribbon for you father," Clara said. She walked over and handed it to Elliot.

A stout man with bright red hair entered the room. "It's a bonny day for a wedding." His cheerfulness was almost contagious. "Clara tells me you two are here to get hitched."

"Yes," Juliette said. "We've traveled for days. I can't wait for our marriage to begin."

Grayson couldn't agree more. "I'm the Duke of

Kissinger," he introduced himself. "You must be Clara's husband, Fergus."

"Ah you're one of those grand lords the English like to boast about," he nodded. "And, aye, I'm Fergus."

Grayson nodded at him. "Now that everyone is accounted for. Will you please perform the ceremony now?"

Elliot didn't answer him immediately. He tinkered around the room until he gathered everything he'd been searching for. He placed all the items on a small table. He set a candle on the table and gestured for them to join him. "All right let's see if we have everything we need to perform your ceremony." He tapped the candle, a quill, a nearby book, and the bright blue ribbon, then turned toward them. "Will you be giving the lass a ring."

He'd forgotten about the betrothal ring. Grayson reached in his inside pocket and pulled out a velvet pouch. With a quick movement he untied a string and dumped it into Elliot's outstretched palm. The gems sparkled in the candlelight. Juliette's gaze remained riveted on it. She glanced up at him, surprise shining out of her eyes.

"Now we are ready to begin..."

CHAPTER 8

The ring glistened in Elliot's hand. She was mesmerized by the sparkling gems. What had made Grayson think she needed something so extravagant? It was lovely, but too much. Her heart thudded inside her chest. This was it—they were about to join themselves together in marriage. Was it a mistake? A part of her wondered if it all would have turned out differently if they'd continued as friends. Maybe they weren't supposed to find their way back to each other. When she was with him it felt so right. She glanced up at him and relaxed. His focus was on Elliot and his preparations for the wedding ceremony. He didn't seem concerned about anything. Doubts were bound to cross her mind from time to time. It was human nature, but she suppressed them. Juliette wanted to spend the rest of her days with Grayson. He was the only man she'd ever had a connection with.

"Before we begin," Elliot said. "I'll need you to remove your gloves."

Juliette stared down at her hands. At least it was warm in the smithy's home, but she felt naked without them. She didn't want to remove them. Grayson picked up one of her hands and said, "Let me."

He slowly unbuttoned the end and peeled one glove off. His touch sent shivers up her arm. She suppressed the need to shiver as tingles filled her belly. After he finished removing the glove he set it aside and repeated the action with the other one. When he was done with his task he let go of her hand. She immediately missed his warmth and wanted to beg him to touch her again.

"Now I need you both to join me in front of this table. Face me and follow my lead." Elliot motioned for them to come forward. He picked up the ribbon Clara had brought to him. He held it in front of him fully stretched out. It was a long thin piece of blue silk. With careful precision he created a small loop on one end, and then pulled the right side through, repeating the action several times. Juliette lost track of how many times he pulled the strip through. After he was done he presented it to them.

"This knot represents love. True love ties us in a way that we can never escape from. It is all encompassing, binding, and integrates deep within our soul. We live and breathe it as it becomes an integral part of us." The knot had somehow formed the shape of a heart as he adjusted it. "Your heart beats for the other person, and vice versa. Life without them is unimaginable." He began working the other side of the ribbon, forming another intricate knot.

Juliette watched in amazement as he worked the fabric to his will. She didn't fully understand the symbolism this one represented, but it fascinated her. Having something else to keep her focus on helped to calm her anxiety, and let her emotions shine through in a different way. She turned her head and glanced up at Grayson. Yes, they were meant to be together, now and forever. She shouldn't question the how or why of anything.

"This knot represents eternity," He explained. "Two souls who wish to spend out their lives together join both love and their lifespan as one."

Elliot gestured toward Grayson and Juliette. "Please face each other."

Grayson turned toward her. She met his gaze willingly and she melted inside. It was filled with heat, and promise. What that promise entailed she wasn't entirely sure but she wanted to find out. Elliot lifted her hand and had her hold it palm up, then did the same with Grayson's. He placed the heart knot in her palm. "The woman is the heart of the relationship. A man learns to love by following her lead. She willingly gives her love freely and without expectations. It's a gift a man cannot refuse, even if he desires to." He placed the eternity knot in Grayson's palm. "The man is tasked with caring for that gift for an infinite amount of time. Nothing is too great a task to keep the woman's love whole and strong. Protection keeps them together through all of life's perils. Whether it be times of joy or sadness it will remain. Giving and receiving equally, love will see you both through life. " Elliot turned to light the candle on the table. "An eternal flame to join two hearts, one love, and a lifetime together."

Juliette stared down at the knots resting in their palms. She never imagined a wedding ceremony such as this one. When they set out to Scotland she thought it would be a quick do you take this man to be your husband, and an equally fast assent. This was rather romantic... She hoped Grayson wasn't panicking about it. Outwardly he remained calm and focused on what Elliot was saying. The smithy couldn't have known this wasn't a love match—at least not on Grayson's part. She'd always loved him, but she feared he wasn't capable of loving anyone. He'd had a hard life and that made him skeptical of anything that wasn't tangible. Love couldn't be measured or seen; it had to be taken on faith. Juliette would give him enough love that maybe over time he'd accept it and learn how to love her in return. She wanted a real marriage, but didn't know how to tell him that. Sometime after the ceremony she'd express her wishes.

He picked up the ring and said. "This ring is an outward symbol of your desire to bring your two lives together." He placed the ring in Grayson's palm next to the eternity knot. "May fate be with you always and bless you, and may you be poor in hardships and rich in blessings, more importantly may you both know nothing but happiness."

Grayson stared down at the ring. She didn't know what was going on inside of his head, but she prayed it was all good things. He lifted his head and met her gaze. His lips lifted upward into a reassuring smile.

Elliot turned toward Grayson and said, "Repeat after me: I, Grayson Abbot, the Duke of Kissinger, take thee Lady Juliette Brooks as my wife."

Grayson said the words to her. His voice didn't waver once; the rich timbre filled her ears and put all her fears at ease. He repeated every word Elliot demanded of him and didn't flinch once. The entire time he kept his focus on her as if he somehow realized she needed him to. Warmth spread through her entire body as she realized soon the ceremony would be over and she'd be his.

"Very good, lad," Elliot praised him. "Now it's the lass's turn." He turned toward Juliette and said, "Repeat after me: I, Lady Juliette Brooks, take thee, Grayson Abbot, The Duke of Kissinger, as my husband..."

Juliette followed Grayson's lead. She kept her voice strong and steady as she repeated her vows. Her focus remained firm and solely on him. He was hers from that point and for always. Protection went both ways. She intended to make sure he never doubted how wonderful he was. To her, he was everything and always had been. She'd prove to him he could always count on her. His love was worth fighting for and she'd not stop until he admitted he couldn't live without her. She didn't realize how much she needed him to love her until that moment. Over the years she'd had to learn how to be patient. That skill would be to her benefit while she sought to win his heart. They had a lifetime together, and she'd not waste one minute of it.

"Now lad," Elliot said. "Pick up the ring and place it on her finger." He gestured toward Juliette's free hand. "And say, with this ring I thee wed."

Grayson slid it on her finger and repeated the words, claiming her as his with one final gesture. He kept her hand in his and looked up at Elliot expectantly.

"I now pronounce you man and wife," he said triumphantly." He placed his hand over the center of the ribbon joined across their two palms. "This is your symbol to keep your love strong. Keep the ribbon safe, and your love will endure." He glanced up at Grayson and said, "You may kiss your bride."

She expected a kiss, craved it. This was her one and only chance to have his lips on hers. Grayson made it clear their marriage wouldn't be a real one. So if he didn't kiss her now—she'd never have one. He picked up the ribbon and folded it carefully, then placed it inside his coat pocket. He turned toward her and smiled. He lifted her hand and kissed the bare back. Tiny sparks of sensation spread through her at the touch of his lips on her. It wasn't what she wanted though, it wasn't a true kiss. This was his way of setting the path their marriage was to take. She had to figure out a way to have him kiss her for real. Not this chivalrous way, it wasn't who he was... What happened to the rake and seducer he was rumored to be? She wanted that Grayson to come out to play.

"That's it?" She raised an eyebrow. "I expected much more than that."

He didn't bother to reply. His attention turned to Elliot. "Are we done?"

"Not quite yet," Elliot replied. "I need to fill out the registry and have you both sign it, along with Clara and Fergus." He gestured for them toward a chair. "Take a seat while I finish up."

Elliot picked up the quill and ink and opened the book. It seemed like he wrote forever before he gestured toward Clara and Fergus to come to him. They each took their turn at the book signing their name to the registry. Juliette fidgeted waiting for her turn to sign the book. Her feet bounced underneath her skirts with anxiety. This had to be completed so proof would remain of their marriage. Without it the union could be challenged. She would remain anxious until it was completed.

"It's your turn lass," Elliot motioned for her to join him. "Sign here." He pointed to a spot on the page. She picked up the quill and placed her signature on the line. A sense of relief went through her as Grayson joined her and signed it as well. It was official—they were husband and wife.

"Thank you," Grayson said. He pulled out enough to pay him for the service. "The ceremony was lovely."

"If there is time, I believe in doing it right. The two of you appear to love each other deeply, and deserved a real wedding." He picked up a piece of parchment and handed it to Grayson. "This is a marriage certificate. In case it's needed. If you need me to verify any of it please let me know."

Grayson nodded and turned toward Juliette, "Well, Your Grace." His lips tilted upward. "I believe that's our cue to let these lovely people enjoy their evening in peace. Let's go back to the inn and rest. I believe you promised I could sleep a whole night through."

She laughed. "That's not how I recall it."

"Oh?" He lifted a brow. Grayson opened the

smithy's door and helped her outside. "Then please tell me what you said."

"I don't believe I mentioned you having a whole night of sleep, you decided to join me as I fell into that blissful state."

This was the side of Grayson she enjoyed. He was happy, carefree, and playful. Maybe the rake would join her in bed that evening—for more than a good night's rest. For their marriage to be indisputable they should consummate it. Perhaps she should point that out.

"I believe you're correct," he agreed. "It's good of you to allow me to encroach on your plans."

They strolled toward the inn and stopped when they noticed the driver waving at them. "Didn't he have something important to tell you?"

Grayson nodded. "I'll speak with him. Go inside the inn and have the innkeeper show you to our room." He kissed the top of her head. "This shouldn't take long."

Juliette nodded and went inside. She found the innkeeper immediately and he had one of the maids escort her to her room. A steaming hot bath greeted her. An idea formed in her head, one that should get Grayson's attention. Maybe this was his plan all along... If he were to find her in her bath it would be a good excuse to abandon his declaration of a name only marriage. Who was she to deny him that excuse? After all she wanted to make love to him and have a real marriage.

Juliette removed her attire and stepped into the bath. It shouldn't be too long before he returned...

CHAPTER 9

Grayson waited for Juliette to go inside before he approached the driver. He didn't want to give her any reason to worry. The driver was practically bounding on the heels of his feet. Whatever news he had to impart was dire enough to make the man anxious. That couldn't be good.

"What is the problem?" he asked.

"There are men here searching for Lady Juliette," he replied. "They were questioning the stable hands."

It was as he expected. Her father had leaped to the conclusion Juliette had ran away to marry. At least he could rest easy with the actual ceremony over. Although it hadn't been consummated, and that technicality could give her father room to question the validity of the marriage. His ridiculous demand it be a marriage in name only was coming back to haunt him. How was he to explain this to his new wife? He'd wanted to change the nature of their marriage, but had hoped to ease her into the idea. She was exhausted from their journey and now he had to be a cad and demand his right to bed her. It was either that or battle her father every step of the way. He'd not take that chance with Juliette's life. It was clear her father had no idea what was best for her or he'd not have sought to tie her to Lord Payne.

"Is it only her they are seeking, or do they realize she is traveling with me?"

The more information he had the better his chances were of protecting her. Afterwards he'd go up to their room and try to explain it all to her. She deserved the truth, and he'd make sure he was always honest with her. He was far from perfect, but for her he'd make an effort to be what she needed. When she came to him for help he'd scoffed at the idea. Now he couldn't imagine a better fate for him. The wedding ceremony had taken him aback at first. It was more meaningful than he expected from an elopement to Gretna Green. The smithy had a romantic heart or perhaps he saw more than either Grayson or Juliette did. Was there a chance they could find love together? The idea of such an emotion hadn't ever occurred to him. Love was for other people, not him.

"No, Your Grace," the driver said. "They assume she is with a man, but the identity of him is unknown. They are focusing their queries to her description and saying she may be with a man."

"Good," he replied. "If they question you attempt to steer them in a different direction. I don't want them disturbing us tonight. I will deal with everything in the morning. My wife deserves a night free from worry and to rest."

"Very well, Your Grace." He nodded. "Will you need anything else from me tonight?"

"No," he said. "Don't hesitate to let me know if there is something requiring my attention before morning. If all else fails err on the side of caution. My wife's safety is my upmost concern." What if it wasn't her father looking for her? He still found it odd Lord Payne had been willing to marry Juliette. What had he gained from the match? If it had been important to him he'd want to prevent her from marrying elsewhere. "While you're looking into it find out who it is exactly that is searching for my wife. I assume it's her father, but I don't want any surprises."

He nodded. "I will keep vigilant on the matter."

"Goodnight," Grayson said. "Have the carriage ready at first light. The sooner we leave for home the better. I hope to avoid any entanglements and arrive at my country seat without any incident."

The driver nodded and headed toward the stable, where he'd bed down for the evening. Grayson returned his attention to the inn. Juliette waited for him in their room. He wasn't sure if he should return to her side now, or give her more time to prepare for bed. He'd ordered a bath for her and she should be taking advantage of it. If he returned too soon he might interrupt her, and as much as he'd like to see her in all her glory—he didn't want to embarrass her either. He respected her too much to take advantage of her, or the situation.

He'd always cared about Juliette, and he supposed he'd loved her in his own way. Albeit, not in a romantic sense, but perhaps he'd been wrong. Maybe that was why he'd always kept tabs on her. He'd wanted to have some connection to her even if he believed he couldn't have her himself. Now that she belonged to him he refused to ever let her go. She might be all right with having a real marriage. He hoped so anyway, especially as she wasn't the one who'd foolishly demanded it. She'd probably expected to share a bed with him. It was a risk she'd been willing to take by asking him to marry her. No doubt it was one of the things she weighed her choices against.

Dawdling outside wasn't helping him make any decisions. He should go inside the inn and at least get warm in the main room. After that he could make a decision to join her immediately, or wait until he believed she'd fallen asleep. He stepped through the entrance and was grateful for the heat that welcomed him. The innkeeper greeted him as soon as he noticed his entrance.

"Your wife is settled in your chamber. Would you like me to have a maid show you to your room?" he asked.

"Not yet," he replied. "Can you have a meal sent up?"

"Yes, Your Grace," he said. "We have a mutton stew and bread. It's not much…"

"It'll do," he replied. "Send up something warm to drink as well, and I'll have a mug of ale now in the common room."

The innkeeper nodded. "Aye, Your Grace," he replied. "Let me know when you'd like to be shown up to your room. For now I'll have a maid bring your wife a meal."

Satisfied he'd done his duty and ensured Juliette would be taken care of he headed into the main room. He found a seat near the hearth and reveled in the warmth. A few moments later a server brought him a mug of ale. He still hadn't decided if he was going to join Juliette after her bath or much later. By his estimation he still had time to make a decision. Ladies took their time with their ablutions.

He took a sip of his ale and almost spit it back in the cup. It was a watered down mess that barely made it fit to consume. Grayson stared at the contents and considered his option: finish the ale, set it aside and ignore it, or just give in and find his room. It was where he wanted to be.

"What brings you to Scotland of all places? Please tell me you're not here to elope. You've sworn off marriage as long as I've known you."

Grayson turned and found Lord Payne standing directly behind him. He was at a loss for words, and really hated his assumption had been correct. The viscount had a reason for wanting Juliette—one he feared he'd not like much.

"Marriage isn't for everyone," Grayson replied evasively. "Although I have friends who swear by it."

Lord Payne laughed. "I should've known you wouldn't be caught in the parson's trap." He clapped him on the shoulder. "Now, I believe marriage will suit me fine. As soon as I take care of some unfinished business here I'm heading to London to sign a betrothal contract."

That was good news of a sort. He hadn't signed the contract yet so he had no legal claim on Juliette. It was something he could work with. Since he wasn't officially tied to her, the viscount couldn't demand he take her back to her father. Grayson, as her husband, could legally tell him to go to hell.

"What business do you have here?"

Grayson had an idea why the viscount was in Gretna Green, but he wanted a confirmation. Juliette was his to protect, and Payne was the reason they'd rushed to Scotland to be married. If he was looking for her it couldn't be a good thing.

"My intended ran away from home. As I was close to the border her father asked me to see if she headed in this direction. I've been here a couple of days and she hasn't made an appearance. She must have gone elsewhere."

Did the man not wonder why Juliette would have run away? It had to be a clue that she didn't desire the match, and yet he was here searching for her. "You sure you want a wife who has a penchant for disappearing?"

"She'll come around after we're wed. All women are rebellious at first." He laughed maniacally. "They need a firm hand to tame them. I know how to handle her. Don't worry about me—I'm rather looking forward to it."

Grayson had an idea how he planned on bringing his intended to heel. The viscount's penchant for beating his lovers was well known in certain circles. He'd been banned from a few of the more prominent establishments for that very reason. It was those clubs that Grayson learned of the man's more sadistic tastes. One of the women had been beaten so bad she nearly died.

He'd told Juliette he'd not marry her at first, but one mention of the viscount and his heart froze in his chest. No woman deserved to find themselves the subject of Lord Payne's attention, but Juliette wasn't just anyone to him. She'd been his best friend when he was denied any close attachments. The very fact she'd come to him for help should've been enough. It shouldn't have taken Lord Payne's name rolling off her tongue to gain his notice. The viscount would never come near her. He'd make sure of it one way or the other. At least Payne was giving up on finding her in Scotland. Perhaps he would depart before them. Grayson would ensure Juliette stayed in their room either until Payne left, or their carriage was ready for them.

"You must want to marry her a great deal if you're here looking for her." Grayson drew his brows together. "What do you get out of this marriage? It can't be a love match if she's off hiding from it."

Not to mention it wouldn't exactly be a cordial environment after the wedding...

"She is to inherit some substantial property, it was part of her mother's dowry," he said. "There was a stipulation in the contracts it must be passed onto one of her children. Unfortunately she only had a daughter—so it became the selling point in marrying her off. I'm rather short on funds and with the income from the property and the yearly stipend I should sit nicely."

"Gah, I can't imagine having to marry for money." Grayson shuddered. "You poor sod."

Whatever woman he married would be the one Grayson would feel sorry for. He was glad he was able to save Juliette from that fate.

"Well, we all can't have the money you do," he said. "We do what we have to survive."

"I wish you luck finding your bride-to-be," Grayson said evenly. He didn't want Payne to know how disgusted he was with him. "It's been a long day, and the ale is rather hideous. I'm off to retire for the evening."

Grayson stood and turned to leave. He didn't take a step before the viscount caught his attention.

"You never did say why you were here," Lord Payne said.

He cursed inwardly. How was he to explain why he was at Gretna Green of all places? There weren't too many reasons for an Englishman to be in the Scottish border town, and all of them resolved around marriage one way or the other. He should be there to either prevent a marriage, or to have one performed. Should he tell Payne the truth? Would he even believe it?

"No, I didn't." Grayson said. His lips lifted into a cocky smile. "And I don't believe I owe you an explanation either. My reasons are my own." He tilted his head slightly. "Good night, Payne."

Grayson didn't want to wait around and leave Payne room to interrogate him further. The sooner he put distance between them the better. The only problem he could see is he had no clue where his room was. Why had he decided to lounge around in the main room? He should have gone upstairs immediately. So much for allowing Juliette some space...

He found a serving girl and asked for directions

to his room. She gestured for him to follow and led him to his chamber. "Thank you," he said, and entered.

Grayson shouldn't have worried about disturbing Juliette. She was fast asleep already on top of the bed, and hadn't even bothered to climb underneath the blankets. At least she'd been able to find a night-gown in the trunk he'd had his staff prepare for her. He lifted her gently and rolled the blanket down beneath her, then placed her back on the bed to spread it over top of her. Damn she was beautiful, even more so in her sleep.

A flash of light caught his attention. He pushed the top of her nightgown over slightly to reveal a gold chain. It seemed familiar... Grayson lifted it and gasped as recognition hit. It was the locket he'd given her at their final Christmas together. She'd kept it— he hadn't expected her to. All right perhaps he believed she'd tossed it in a box and forgotten about it, but never would he have believed she still wore it.

What did it mean?

In the morning he'd have to ask her. It could be he was reading too much into the gesture, but in his heart he hoped it meant they had a future together. For now he'd lay beside her and rest. Tomorrow was soon enough to begin their future together.

CHAPTER 10

Juliette rolled onto her side and hit a solid mass. What was in her bed? She'd been dreaming of her last Christmas with Grayson. It had been lovely and it warmed her from the inside out. If they could capture that feeling and hold onto it tightly she'd never feel lonely ever again.

At least until reality reared its ugly head. She opened her eyes and found him asleep next to her. When had he come back? She'd given up on him returning while she was in her bath. It had gotten cold too fast, and on the trip to Scotland she'd found she'd abhorred any frigid temperature. There had been two trunks waiting in the room along with her bath. Grayson had mentioned the last time they'd stayed at an inn he'd arranged for her to have clothing. This was her first opportunity to rummage through the trunks offerings. She'd sighed in relief to find a clean dressing gown, and a brush. As much as she wanted to wait for him to return her exhaustion overtook her. She only meant to lay down for a moment, and that was the last thing she recalled.

Grayson must have come back and found her fast asleep. He'd probably been relieved. Did he expect she'd demand he make her his wife in truth? They were legally wed, but he'd never love her. Not in any way that mattered. She'd like to have children some day, and he apparently hadn't cared if she took a lover. Somehow she doubted he'd been truthful then. There had been a strange gleam in his eye that made her wonder what he'd really been thinking, but hadn't wanted to press the issue.

Now that they were wed, she'd push harder. She wasn't sure how to make him see that marriage to her would make him happy. Somehow she'd have to find the patience to see it all through. Juliette was determined to persevere.

"Good morning," he said huskily. "Did you sleep well?"

"I did," she replied. Her cheeks warmed. They'd been in each other's company for days, but somehow this seemed more intimate. They'd never awoken beside each other in a bed before.

He lifted his hand and ran it down her side, and rested it on her hip. "We need to talk, but it can wait until we're dressed. Do you want me to give you privacy?"

What could they have to discuss? The marriage was done. He'd not made love to her, and it didn't appear he planned to. Maybe there was something they had to talk about. What was their next step? Would they return to London or to his country seat? How was she going to explain all of this to her father?

"You can stay," she said. Juliette lowered her gaze. She didn't want him to see how nervous she was. "There's a privacy screen I can make use of."

He lifted her chin and forced her to look in his eyes. "You don't need to hide from me." Grayson lowered his hand and skimmed his fingers across her neck. It rested on the gold chain she always wore. Juliette blushed and started to move away. How could she have forgotten she was wearing it? She'd been so careful to keep the locket hidden—hadn't wanted him to realize how much he still meant to her.

"Don't pull away," he demanded. His fingers

skimmed the chain and he pulled the locket into his palm. He pressed the latch and it slipped open with a slight click. Inside he'd find the miniature portrait of him as a boy. If she'd been able to update it to a more recent one she would have. It was enough to have a piece of him resting against her heart every day. "Why do you still wear this?"

There was a small hitch in his voice—it cracked a little as he asked the question. Did it bother him she still had the locket? "It's a piece of my past that I don't want to forget. A happier time that I'll never have again."

"What if you could?" He pulled her into his arms and rested his forehead against hers. His eyes remained closed. She didn't know what he was asking of her, none of it made sense. What did the locket have to do with anything? He pulled back and his eyelids fluttered open. "You smell so good. I want nothing more than to kiss you—taste you the way I've been craving since the first time I saw the woman you'd grown into."

"That was days ago. What's been stopping you?"

He shook his head. "That wasn't the first time I saw you in the past fifteen years."

When had he seen her? She didn't go out in society, and hadn't since before her mother died. Even then it had been a mere two weeks, and except for her come out ball she'd hugged the wall. No one had wanted to be her friend. The gentlemen were nicer at her first official ball. Since it had been thrown in her honor she'd had plenty of dance partners.

"I don't understand," she said. "If you saw me why didn't you come and talk to me. I'd have loved to have had some time with you. Where was this?"

Grayson didn't answer right away. She didn't know why he was holding back, and she was a fool. He'd said he wanted to kiss her and she'd stupidly turned into an inquisitor instead of demanding he put his lips on hers. Now she'd have to wait even longer to find out if it was as wonderful as she'd imagined.

"I was invited to your ball," he finally said. "My father forbade me to go. He did that a lot while he was alive." Grayson closed his eyes again and sighed. "He didn't like how close we'd become. I was usurping the plans he had for me, and he was making sure I followed the path he set for me. That's why I had to stay away from you, but I couldn't resist seeing you. I didn't know when I'd have the chance again. So I sneaked inside through a back entrance—I couldn't be announced formally. I watched you dance and laugh. It hurt, but I was glad you were so happy. After that I kept my distance."

Her heart beat rapidly inside of her chest. He did care about her, and always had. This was something she had been wanting to hear for so long. Damn his father for keeping them apart. Their lives might be so different if he'd not been hell bent on controlling his son. "Kiss me," she demanded.

Grayson cupped her cheek in his hand and lowered his mouth to hers. His lips were warm and soft. It was sweet at first, but it quickly changed to something far more than that. His hand left her face and roamed down her shoulders until they rested on her hip. Juliette wanted more—of him. He pulled her against him and ran kisses down her cheek and then her neck. She squirmed in his arms simultaneously pushing at him and wanting to crawl as close to him as possible.

Kisses were marvelous things and she'd never have enough of them.

"Gray," she said breathlessly. "I love you."

He groaned and pulled her on top of him. "Don't say it if you don't mean it."

Why would she do something so heinous? "I wouldn't do that to you. You mean too much to me."

She caressed his cheek. "You don't have to say it back, but I hope one day you will."

Grayson pushed his hands into her dark tresses and pulled her down to him. There gazes were locked together, and their lips just short of touching. "You don't have to wait for me to say those words to you. I've always loved you. You've owned my heart since we were children, but what I felt for you then doesn't compare to what's in my heart now. What's between us is as real as anything out there, and I look forward to making a lifetime of memories with you." He closed the distance between them and kissed her again. Passion ignited between them.

Juliette lost all thought and just reveled in the feel of his body against hers. The kisses, touches, and loving were all more pleasure than she could imagine. They hadn't had a wedding night, but Grayson made up for it with a morning she'd never forget... He made sure there would be no doubt she was his wife, and Juliette couldn't have been happier if she tried...

GRAYSON SHOULD'VE WAITED to make love to Juliette, but he'd never been a patient man. Besides with Lord Payne hovering around the inn it was for the best. Afterwards they'd lingered in bed as long as he dared let them. The sooner they headed back to London the better. Originally he intended to take her to Kissinger, but it was better if he dealt with her father first. They couldn't have anything being held over their head—not if they wanted to have a happy life together.

So he rolled out of bed and dressed before he was tempted to love her all over again, then he helped her with her gown. Dressing her was almost as much fun as he imagined it would be to take the gown off her. He placed kisses all over her as he buttoned it up.

Juliette laughed. "You're rather good at this."

"This is only the beginning, darling," he whispered in her ear. "We have a lifetime for me to explore you, and I intend to take my husbandly duties seriously." He brushed back her dark curls and kissed her shoulder. " Do you need help with your hair too?"

"Shoo," she said. "I will pin my hair up myself. It will be done much faster without your attentions. Go see to the coach and have our trunks taken to the carriage."

Grayson spun her around to face him. He leaned down and kissed her with all the love in his heart.

She matched his kiss with equal fervor. When he pulled back he felt the loss of her heat, but was pleased with how plump her lips remained from their shared passion. "Something for you to think about while I'm gone."

"You're wicked," she said breathlessly. "I like this side of you. I'm glad you're mine."

He kissed her forehead and said. "Stay here until I come and get you. It is safer for you here."

She scrunched up her nose. "What danger could possibly be lurking in the inn?"

"Jules..."

She held up her hand and interrupted him. "Don't bother telling me about protecting me and all that nonsense. It's going to take me a while to pin my hair up anyway. I'm sure by the time the horses are hitched to the carriage and the trunks ready to be loaded I'll be finished with it. So go take care of business and leave me be."

He didn't bother arguing with her. She was probably right. Her hair would take a while to properly fix. "Miss me while I'm gone."

"Always," she said.

Grayson left her to her task and went down to the main room. He left the inn and went to the stable first. The carriage hadn't been outside and he wanted to find out what the delay was. He found his driver inside wrestling with one of the horses.

"Will the carriage be ready soon?"

"Yes, Your Grace," he replied. "One of the horses went lame and I had to trade her for a new mount. He's being a little feisty about joining the team. I'll have him ready soon enough. The carriage should be out front at half past the hour."

"That's good. I'd like to leave as soon as possible. The sooner I'm out of Scotland the happier I'll be." He studied the horse giving the driver a hard time. "I'll ask the innkeeper to provide some lads to help with the trunks. You have your work cut out for you with this beast."

"Thank you," he replied. "I appreciate it."

Grayson nodded and left the driver to deal with harnessing the horses to the carriage. The morning had gone better than he'd hoped. Juliette loved him. As far as he was concerned all was right in the world. Soon they'd be on their way and headed back to London, albeit much slower than their journey to Scotland. No reason to rush back.

He found innkeeper immediately. He was writing something in his register. "Can you have some lads help load my trunks onto my carriage?"

"Of course, Your Grace," he said. "I trust you had a pleasant rest?"

"I did," he replied. "Best night sleep I've had in days."

"Good." The innkeeper beamed. "And your wife?"

"I didn't realize you'd married," Payne said from behind him.

Grayson closed his eyes and cursed silently. Why hadn't he left already?

"No reason you would," Grayson said calmly. "I didn't shout it to the world I'd intended to wed."

He prayed Payne didn't ask who he'd married. If he didn't realize Juliette was his wife he might let it go and leave him in peace. What were the chances of that happening?

"What lucky lady did you make your duchess?"

"That would be me," Juliette said, and then glanced at Grayson. "I finished much quicker than I thought. It was boring sitting by myself. How long until we leave."

Christ. Why hadn't she stayed in the room? Maybe Payne wouldn't realize who she was. As if that was possible. Hadn't his driver mentioned he had a description of her to show people?

Payne looked at Juliet and then back at Grayson.

He noticed when the realization hit the viscount. He barely managed to avoid being hit by the man's wild punch. "You bastard," he screamed. "You knew last night didn't you."

Grayson took a step back. "Jules do me a favor and go back to the room."

"What is happening?" she asked. "Why is he trying to hit you?"

"She was supposed to be mine," Payne exclaimed.

Juliette's gaze flew to the viscount, and then back at Grayson. Her mouth formed opened wide on a silent oh. That's right—he wanted to scream at her. Lord Payne had planned on marrying her, and now he planned on taking on Grayson for daring to take her away from him.

"Gentlemen," the innkeeper said. "We don't allow fighting in the inn. Take this outside immediately."

Grayson turned to Juliette and said, "Stay in here. You'll be safer." Then walked out of the inn, Viscount Payne was a short distance behind. It would be better if they didn't brawl at all, but at least outside they'd be less likely to damage any of the inn's property. Grayson walked a fair enough distance from the inn, to the side of the entrance and stopped.

"Payne," Grayson said. "We don't have to do this. I have a prior relationship with Juliette that supersedes yours." He shrugged. "Besides we both know you don't have an actual claim. You didn't sign the betrothal contract."

Payne's face turned beet red and his lips curled up in displeasure. "I should've realized last night why you were here. You wouldn't tell me, but I figured that was you being you. But now that I've had time to think about it—your estate borders her fathers. How long have you been bedding her?"

Grayson couldn't listen to him discuss Juliette's virtue in vulgar terms. She was innocent of any wrong doing, and he'd not touched her in that way until after they'd married. His fist hit Payne's face before he realized what he was doing. The viscount hit the ground with a loud thud.

Viscount Payne wiped a drop of blood from his nose, and then slowly returned to his feet. "For that I'm going to enjoy killing you." He pulled a pistol out of his pocket and aimed it at Grayson. "You're correct. I don't have a claim—yet but that can be rectified. With you gone she'll be free once again. No need to bother with a mourning period. Her father doesn't need to know about this unfortunate turn of events."

Grayson froze and considered his options. Viscount Payne planned to murder him and return to London with Juliette as if nothing had happened. The man had lost his mind. "And what if she's already carrying my child? Are you going to claim it as your own?"

He hadn't thought about the possibility of a child. Grayson hadn't ever believed he'd be a father, but everything was different with Juliette. She made the unattainable seem possible. For her he'd fight with every breath in his body. The viscount would not have a chance to sully her in any way.

"There are ways to rid a woman of a babe." He shrugged. "If it turns out she's enceinte I'll deal with it."

Horror froze Grayson's tongue in his mouth. If he did as he proposed—it could kill Juliette, but why should he care about murdering a mother and child? Clearly the idea of ending a person's life didn't bother him as he was fully prepared to shoot Grayson. The time for thinking was at an end, and actions had to be taken to stop his evil. Grayson leapt at Payne and fought for control of the pistol. It went off, the echo ricocheting through the air. Viscount

Payne's scream followed shortly after, and then he slumped to the ground in a heap, the pistol lying out of his reach.

Grayson wanted to be sorry, but he couldn't. The man had threatened him, and his wife. The constable would have to be called to handle the situation. Payne wasn't dead, but he was gravely injured. He'd go to the inn and have them take care of him. A doctor would need to be sent for. He turned to head to the inn and halted. Juliette and the innkeeper were standing not far in the distance. How long had they been watching?

"I was frightened. I didn't know it was Lord Payne you were talking to. He was the last person I expected to see here." Juliette ran to him and hugged him tight in her embrace.

That partially was his fault. He should have told her the viscount was in Scotland searching for her. A lesson learned the hard way—he'd not keep anything from her ever again. It could lead to disastrous results.

"It's all right," he said soothingly.

"Is he dead?" The innkeeper asked.

"No," Grayson shook his head. "But he might be if he doesn't get some care. Can you take care of everything for me?"

The innkeeper nodded. "Aye, I'll see to everything. The constable will have questions, but I'll give him your direction."

"Thank you," Grayson said. "I appreciate it."

"The lass and I saw everything. The man's intentions were clear. You're entitled to defend yourself." He stared at Viscount Payne's prone form. "He got what he deserved."

Viscount Payne was capable of a lot of evil. He'd hoped to protect Juliette from it. Maybe now they could go on and not think about what the viscount might do. He would be facing the constable, and whatever charges he seemed fit. They could put the whole fiasco in the past and move forward. He hugged Juliette against him and said, "We're leaving as soon as the trunks are loaded in the carriage."

She nodded and let him lead her to their carriage, and supervised the loading of the trunks. Grayson kept her close by his side until it was time to depart. It didn't take long for the carriage to be ready. They were settled in the carriage and well on their way out of Scotland before he breathed a sigh of relief.

"You too?" She asked.

"What?"

"Viscount Payne," she shuddered. "He meant to

kill you. I'm relieved to leave him behind and head home."

"I couldn't agree more," he said. "I wasn't sure I'd make it out of that situation alive, but I had to do everything I could because the alternative was unacceptable. He would have hurt you, and I couldn't allow that."

"I never want to go through that again. It's made me realize something else to." She laid her hand on his chest and met his gaze. "It's been an adventure, and while I look forward to our life together—I want to stay home for a while. I've discovered I don't particularly enjoy excitement as much as I thought I would."

"So my plans for our wedding trip to Rome are out?" He hadn't actually made any plans. Where would he have found the time? But he couldn't help teasing her. "I had high hopes of finding out if I compared to your fantasies about those gladiators."

Juliette scrunched her nose up. "Maybe one day, but as long as your with me, I'm content. We don't need to go anywhere."

He leaned down and kissed her lightly. "My heart is happiest with you near too."

"There was a time I believed no gentlemen would want to kiss me. Wallflowers find it hard to imagine a happily-ever-after. " Her whole face brightened as she met his gaze. "But now I know I was waiting for you. No other man's kiss would have been right."

He'd kiss her every day, more than once if necessary, if that was her desire. But this year would always hold a special place in his heart. It was their first one as husband and wife, and kissing Juliette was a gift he'd always hold dear. Christmastide hadn't gone as he'd planned—it'd been so much better...

EPILOGUE

Grayson was sitting in his study going over some of the paperwork his steward had sent over for him to examine. So far he hadn't found anything out of the ordinary and wasn't sure why the man thought it needed his attention. He had to be missing something, but finding it was proving impossible. He'd have to leave it for another day.

Christmastide had started and he'd promised Juliette he'd spend the evening with her. It was the anniversary of their first year as husband and wife. It was a celebration he hoped to cherish every year. Not every man had the pleasure of loving his wife. Grayson considered himself lucky he'd married her. He'd almost been foolish enough to refuse.

He set the papers on his desk in a neat pile.

They'd wait for him there. When the time was right he'd look them over with fresh eyes, and possibly then he'd figure out what his steward wanted him to see. He flipped through a set of invitations—only one peaked his interest. It was from his good friend the Marquis of Knightly and his wife. The invitation was for him and Juliette to attend a dinner they were holding over Christmastide. It was an intimate affair that would only have their closest friends in attendance. Grayson assumed it would include Bradford, the marchioness's brother, along with her friend Pippa and her husband. He scribbled a quick note to be delivered accepting the invite on behalf of himself, and Juliette. He couldn't wait to see his friends and hoped everyone would be there.

For now he'd go in search of Juliette. Grayson left his study and headed to the sitting room. They'd chosen to spend the season at his London townhouse. That way she could remain close to her father. The earl had been more worried about Juliette than angry, and welcomed her home with open arms. He'd been surprised she'd run away to marry Grayson. Her father hadn't realized just how opposed Juliette had been to marrying Lord Payne, and apologized for not listening to her, and following Eloise's advice. For her part, Juliette was glad she didn't have to see her step-mother every day. There would never be any love between the two women, but they'd learn to tolerate each other for the earl's sake. Riverdale had been horrified to learn of Lord Payne's crimes. Payne survived his injury and was deported for his actions. His title had been stripped from him and given to the next person in line to inherit it. In the end it had all worked out.

When he entered the sitting room he found Juliette staring out a window. It was similar to the memory of their last Christmastide as children. She even had a similar expression on her face. Her eyes were wide, her mouth opened a touch, and her cheeks slightly reddened.

"Wishing on stars again are you?"

Juliette turned from the window and faced him. "Not many stars to see in the city." She crossed the room to him and wrapped her arms around him in an embrace. He held her against him as she laid her head on his shoulder. "Besides all my wishes have come true. What could I possibly hope to gain that I don't already have?"

He kissed the top of her head. "What did you wish for all those years ago."

She glanced up at him and met his gaze. "I wished to spend all of my days with you by my side.

It took longer than I expected, but better late than never." Her lips tilted upward. "What would you have wished for."

"The same thing," he replied. "Although I'm more greedy than you. I want more."

His life was more than he could have imagined it could be, and it was all because of her. Happiness had seemed so elusive at one time in his life. Now that he had it he couldn't imagine how he'd managed without it for most of his life. There was only one thing that would make it better.

"Oh?" She raised an eyebrow. "What do you want? Maybe I can give it to you."

"I'm counting on it," he replied. He leaned down and whispered in her ear, "Please make me a father."

She jerked back, surprise filling her eyes. He'd believed he'd make a horrible father. His own had been a terrible role model. The more time he spent with Juliette he believed it could be possible.

"In that case," Juliette said. The corner of her lip twitched. "I have good news for you, Your Grace." She cupped his cheek in her hand. "It's my pleasure to inform you that you will be a father sometime in early summer. I hope that meets with your approval."

He couldn't have asked for anything more. "You're perfect."

When he looked into her eyes every wish he'd ever dared to hope for came true. She was his everything. He'd been a fool and gave up on her. At least she'd had the good sense to come to him in her moment of need. They took the long way around, but it worked out how it was supposed to. She was the brightest part, and the shooting star he'd made the biggest wish of his life on. When she crossed his path again it was the best thing that happened to him. He'd never give up her, on them, ever again.

They'd come so far in their lives. Life could do its worst and throw anything at them, and through it all he'd have faith in the strength of their love. Because Juliette was what held it all together. He finally understood the importance of the knots at their wedding. It was more than a string tied together in a fancy way. It was their love knotted together for eternity, and he wouldn't have it any other way.

EXCERPT: SURRENDERING TO MY SPY

DAWN BROWER

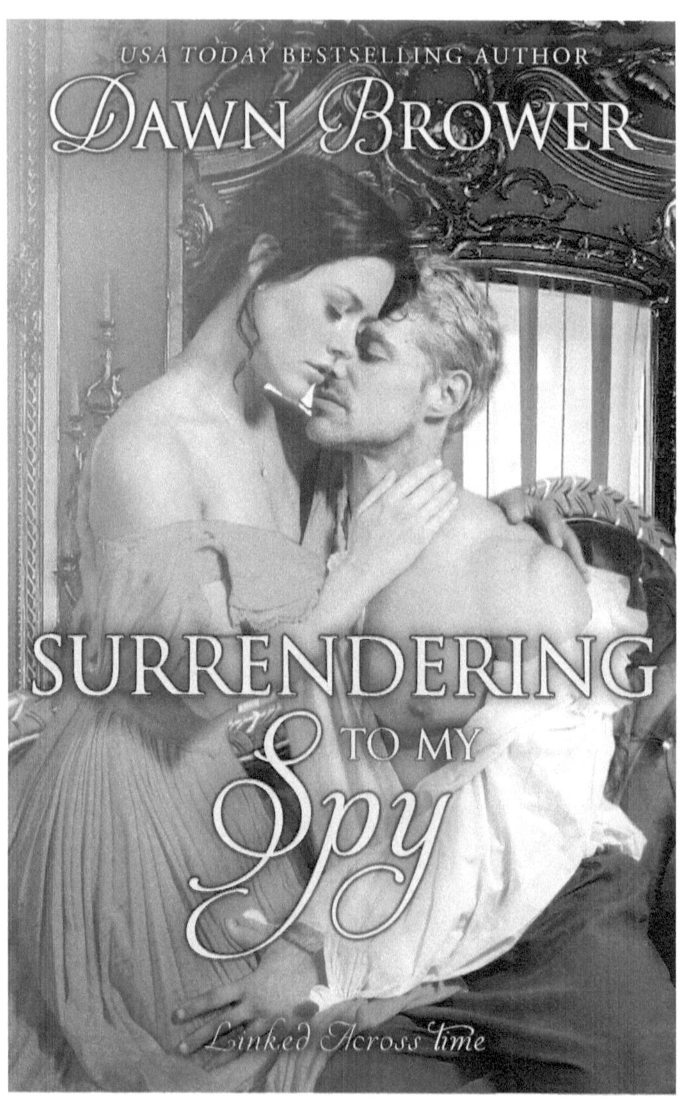
USA TODAY BESTSELLING AUTHOR
DAWN BROWER
SURRENDERING
TO MY
Spy
Linked Across Time

June 1815

Lady Rosanna Kendall strolled down the hall of her brother's townhouse. Her brother, Edward, was the current Duke of Weston. He'd inherited the title a few years past when their father passed on. An echo of voices came through the walls. Rosanna stopped short when she recognized who was speaking with Edward in his study. Lord Seabrook was in there. "Dom," she whispered to herself. Dominic Rossington, the Marquess of Seabrook. She'd loved him from afar most of her life, and he was now a breath away. If she dared to go into the study and interrupt them she'd be able to see him, and if she was lucky enough maybe a touch as well.

Did she dare?

Rosanna inched closer to the room. The door was slightly ajar. She peeked inside and saw movement. A blur of dark fabric and a slight hint of blond hair—nothing more. She wanted to have the full view of Dom's perfection. He had to be the most handsome man in creation. He had glorious golden hair, eyes the color of a stormy gray sky, and the face of an angel. That is if an angel could master the wicked glances the marquess threw out with regularity.

Rosanna was no fool. She knew he was a rogue of the highest accord. He made no secret he wasn't seeking a wife and found what he desired in the arms of many other women. Her heart hurt knowing he'd never love her the same way she did him. It turned out unrequited love would be her lot in life. She shook her melancholy away and focused on their discussion. It wouldn't do to fall into that particular line of thought. Dom would never be hers, and it was time to let the fantasy go. She'd had suitors a plenty, but not one of them measured up to her dream.

"I wish you wouldn't involve yourself in this," Dom said. "James…"

"I don't bloody care what my brother would say," Edward spat out. "I'm the Duke of Weston and I can do whatever I want."

What were they arguing about? What did it have to do with James? Rosanna hadn't seen her other brother, Edward's twin, in a couple of years. He'd joined a Calvary regiment and went off to fight in the war against Napoleon. She was terrified one day they'd receive news of him that wouldn't be good. It was hard to sit with the knowledge he could be gravely injured or—she gulped—die fighting. Dom was James's best friend. If not for their friendship she'd not have had the opportunity to come to know Dom so well. She saw a side of him none of his chosen lovers did. He was funny, protective, and loyal to those he cared for. That was the man she'd fallen in love with. Yes, Rosanna was vain enough to realize it was his face she'd noticed first, but once she'd seen past his blinding beauty and into his soul everything changed.

A loud crash brought her back to reality. It echoed through the room as something thudded against the wall. Rosanna jerked back and clenched her arms against herself.

"You're a fool," Dom shouted. "What you've done..."

"I've done nothing you haven't."

"There is a difference and you better well realize it before you make a mistake you can't return from."

Dom's voice was edged with a hardness Rosanna had never heard before. What had Edward done? "Tell me what you're reckless plan uncovered."

"Not here," Edward said. "You never know who's listening."

What was Edward hiding? What made him so nervous? Should she be worried? Dom appeared to be angry at her brother, and Dom never even remotely raised his voice. He was always carefree and congenial. If Edward didn't want to discuss it at their home—it must be serious. She should leave before they exited the study. They'd both turn their ire on discovering her hovering nearby.

"Something you should have considered before you followed a trail that could lead to your death."

"Don't be so dramatic, Dom. That's unlikely to happen."

Was Dom right? Had Edward done something that could get him killed? She'd been worried for so long about James's safety and perhaps she'd been praying for the wrong brother. Rosanna backed away from the study and headed to the library. It was close enough to Edward's study she'd be able to hear when they left.

She stopped short when she realized the library wasn't empty as she'd assumed. Lady Callista Lyon, the Countess of Marin sat on a nearby settee reading a book. She glanced up as Rosanna entered. Her dark green eyes brightened when she met Rosanna's gaze. Callista was betrothed to her brother, Edward. They were set to be married in a sennight. The wedding was to take place at Weston Manor. The family, along with Callista's, was scheduled to travel there by midweek.

"I'm sorry to disrupt you," Rosanna said. "I thought the library was unoccupied."

"I welcome the intrusion," Lady Callista said and set her book down. "I sent my maid to fetch my cloak. I don't know what is taking your brother so long, but it's past time I went home."

It was rather unusual for her brother's intended to be lounging in their library. What had the lady been thinking? She was rather independent, and a widow, but there was still propriety standards that should be adhered to. She didn't know Lady Callista well. The little she knowledge she had consisted of, a marriage to the elderly Earl of Marin when she was eight and ten. The earl had died a mere six months after the marriage. She'd been out of mourning no more than a month before she caught Edward's eye. It was no surprise why. Lady Callista was a beauty. She had beautiful mahogany hair and the greenest eyes she'd ever seen. Her heart shaped face was exquisite. Rosanna wished she could be as graceful and poised as her. If she were more—approachable. Rosanna didn't feel as if she could truly become close to her. She was friendly enough, but there was something elusive about her as well.

"I have your cloak, milady. Do you wish to depart now?"

"You're leaving?" Edward entered the room. "I didn't realize how late it was. I'm sorry I left you alone."

"It is all right. I entertained myself. We can discuss the wedding plans on the way to your estate in a couple of days." Callista nodded at her maid. The young woman draped it over her with care. "I'll take your leave until then."

Edward nodded. He didn't even spare Rosanna a glance. "I'll see you out."

It was brief and over before she'd even realized what happened. Edward's relationship with Lady Callista was so...odd. She didn't know what it was that bothered her. Perhaps she'd never know. In her experience it was hard to truly know what went on between two people. Only those inside it were truly aware of all the nuances. Maybe one day she'd share that wonder with another.

"What are you doing all alone in here?"

Rosanna turned and met Dom's gaze. She repressed a sigh at the sight of him. This had been what she'd wanted. Some time to stare at his male beauty and to hear his voice in that low tone that sent shivers down her body. She'd never tire of being around him.

"Edward left to escort Lady Callista to the door. I don't rate a glance from my brother these days." She tilted her head and studied him. "What are you doing here?" Perhaps that was insolent, but she couldn't help herself. She'd never stood on formality where Dom was concerned. Why hadn't he left before her brother came into the library? Were they leaving to go somewhere more private to discuss Edward's discovery?

"I have business with your brother, brat." He strolled into the room. "But I can keep you company until he returns."

"It's not necessary." As much as she loved him, and adored being in his company, Rosanna was afraid she'd confess it all in a blubbery mess of need. He turned her insides to mush, and her thoughts weren't far behind. "I am capable of spending time by myself."

His lids drooped low as he stared down at her. "A

beautiful lady shouldn't ever be left to her own devices. What fun would that be?"

Was he? No, he couldn't be. Dom appeared to be flirting with her. What game was he playing? She didn't dare hope he wanted to court her properly. He'd never once indicated an interest in her. He wouldn't start now. There had to be another reason for him speak to her in an overly familiar manner.

"I'm not one of your light skirts," she said harshly. "Don't speak to me as if I were."

Dom stepped back as if she'd slapped him. Color drained from his face. "I'd never..."

"I'd hope not." Rosanna lifted her chin arrogantly. "I plan on marriage, and the entire ton knows how you feel about taking a wife."

"That they do," he said sardonically. He gave her the once over with slow excruciating precision. "I assure you, not only do I never intend to marry, but you're the last lady I'd ever consider."

He spun on his heels and left her alone. His words shattered her heart into thousands of tiny pain filled shards. What had she done? She'd pushed him away forever. Why had she spoken to him with such harshness? He hadn't done anything untoward. Dom —was well—Dom, there wasn't a mean bone in his body. Rosanna would never recover from her blunder.

"LADY ROSANNA," Dominic Rossington, the Marquess of Seabrook said, with a bow. The discord between them remained palpable whenever they were near each other. She'd been so warm and welcoming in the past, but that changed with one flicker of thoughtless words flung in her direction. He should regret them, and in a way he did. It didn't change the circumstances. Rosanna needed to understand he would never marry. He wasn't a fool, and was very much aware of her growing attachment. In a different world he'd have been pleased and delighted at the prospect of having her as a wife. But his life didn't leave room for one. "I apologize for intruding, but I have news I must share with you."

Rosanna was sitting in the library they'd last seen each other in. Had it been two days since he'd laid eyes on her? She was as beautiful as he remembered, and equally as untouchable. Her dark tresses were coiled on top of her head in an elaborate chignon, and her violet eyes observed him with cool efficiency.

"I won't keep you. Tell me what you must as I'm

sure my company disgusts you." Her voice was hoarse with an unidentifiable emotion. "I believe I'm the last person you wish to have any sort of discourse with."

This had to be about his last remark about her being the last lady he'd ever marry. No young lady liked to hear those words thrown at them. Dom had been the worst kind of swine to say them aloud to her. He meant them though, but not for the reasons she assumed. Lady Rosanna Kendall was too good for him. He would taint her by spending any amount of time in her company. She deserved a husband who would cherish and adore her. Someone who didn't have the reputation he'd carefully cultivated over the past few years.

"I promise you, I don't distain you in the slightest." His forehead creased. "You're to go to Weston Manor in the morning, and I had to tell you..."

How could he say it? She'd be devastated once she learned of the news. The whole family would be. What about James? How was he to tell his best friend he was responsible for what happened to Edward. If he'd been able to stop him in his foolhardy inquiries...

"What is it?" Rosanna leaned forward and studied him. "You're not usually at a loss for word."

Dom didn't want to hurt her, had never wanted to do her any kind of harm. The words that were currently lodged in his throat would surely cause her no small amount of pain. But he had to tell her before someone else did. She should hear the news from someone who cared about her and her family.

"There was an accident..."

Rosanna leapt up and strode toward him. "Is it James?"

Of course she'd jump to that conclusion. Why wouldn't it be James? He was at war and on the front lines. He shook his head. "No, it isn't James."

"Who is it?" she demanded. "You're scaring me."

Dom closed his eyes and prayed for strength. Rosanna was the one woman he'd always admired and vowed to take care of. No other had ever mattered as much to him. He'd lay down his life to protect her, and here he was about to destroy a part of her. It had to be done.

"Edward's carriage hit something in the road. A wheel broke and it tipped over the side of a bridge. He—didn't make it to Weston Manor." He stared into her violet eyes and said morosely, "It's with greatest sympathy I must tell you that your brother, Edward, The fourth Duke of Weston, has died."

Rosanna's screams filled his ears. Tears streamed

down her face as she beat her small fists against his chest. He took every bit of her ire as he believed was his due. Dom hadn't protected Edward from his reckless behavior, and now the people he cared about most would pay that price. After a short while he helped her back onto the settee and called for a maid to see to her care. He turned, exited the room, and left her alone—not once glancing back.

Rosanna wasn't his, and never would be...

EXCERPT: A HIDDEN RUBY

DAWN BROWER

DAWN BROWER
A
Hidden
Ruby

PROLOGUE

"I no longer wish to live... Without my love, I have nothing."

Rubina Leone St. John, the Duchess of Huntly meant those words. Without Noah... Her head fell forward hitting the palm of her hands. Tears streamed down her face. How could she go on without the only man she'd ever loved? If Paolo Fonte, Duca d'Sordillo, told the truth, her husband was dead.

"Don't be dramatic, Rubina." He held his hand over his heart. "On my honor, I will always take care of you."

She lifted her head and stared at him through hooded eyes. What a fool. Did he honestly believe she'd willingly stay with him? Her heart would always belong to Noah. No other man would fill the empty void his loss left behind. Slowly, she stood and faced him. With all the strength she had left, she spit in his face.

"You'll never take the place of my Noah." She returned to her seat. Rubina had better things to do with her time than deal with Paolo. He proclaimed to love her, but he'd kept her a prisoner for months in a tiny room. Only coming to visit her so he could stare at her while declaring his love. You don't imprison someone you supposedly love.

Paolo pulled out a handkerchief and wiped his face. "You'll regret that."

"No, I only wish I'd have done it sooner."

He stormed over to her side and lifted her chin, forcing her to look at him.

"*La mia bellezza...*" He stroked his fingers through her hair. "Such beautiful golden-blonde hair —so silky to touch."

Chills ran down her spine and her stomach rolled with queasiness as he touched her. Rubina was not his beauty... She never would be his in any way.

"I don't belong to you. I never have. When will you accept that?" She stared up at him in defiance.

"Never?" He raised an eyebrow. "It is such a very long time, my love. You will learn to love me."

Rubina choked back tears. If Noah was truly dead—it didn't matter. Paolo could do his worst. No matter how hard she tried, her feelings would remain the same. Her heart remained untouched by his false charms...

"*Ti odio.*" She let every ounce of hatred pour out of her. Rubina didn't want there to be any doubt how much she loathed Paolo.

"No, you don't." His sinister laugh filled the tiny room. "My dear, you don't really know what hate is—but you will."

"How did Noah die?"

Rubina needed details to understand how he could really be gone. Her husband was a strong virile man, so full of life. She couldn't truly believe he was—she gulped down a lump in her throat—dead.

"If you must know, someone helped him along to his untimely demise."

"No..." Rubina gasped. "Please—tell me you didn't murder him."

"I'll tell you no such thing. I'm not about to start lying to you my dear." He shoved his hands into his pockets and rocked back on his heels. "It's best you get acclimated to our long life together."

Rubina wanted to die. That would remain true as long as Noah was gone. She had something to take care of before she joined him again. Paolo Fonte's life must end. He would pay for his sins—for hurting Noah. She would live long enough to see it happen. Once she sent him to hell, she'd allow herself to breathe her last breath. She could once again be with her husband. They could spend eternity in each other's arms.

"*Sei un bastardo malvagio,*" she exclaimed. Duca d'Sordillo was an evil bastard. "One day your cruelty will leave this world. On that day I will rejoice."

"Say what you want. Your words mean nothing, but you will come around." He grinned. "Until then, please enjoy the accommodations.

He turned to leave. The door shut with a loud thud. Paolo turned the key, locking her once again in her tiny hovel. Such love he showed her. Rubina stared at the door with disgust. It didn't matter. She had a reason to continue living. Once she found a way to end Paolo's life her mission would be complete. He must pay for the atrocity he caused.

RUBINA GREW WEAK. She barely sustained enough strength to lift up her head. Paolo limited her food to bread and water—barely enough to survive. He was trying to get her to cave—give in to his demands. The evil bastard wanted her to willingly join him in his bed. It would never happen. To betray Noah in such a manner... No, she'd rather die. If she didn't gain strength soon, she'd get her wish.

"Duchessa..."

Her body rocked back and forth, shaking from an unseen force, but she didn't want to open her eyes.

"Please wake up, Duchessa."

Rubina's eyelids fluttered open to gaze into the dark brown eyes of a man she'd never seen before.

"Who are you?" She stared at him, puzzled. Maybe he was a new guard Paolo sent to watch over her.

"I'm here to save you."

Rubina shook and tears streamed down her face. She didn't want to believe it was true. She didn't know how long she'd been a captive in Paolo's home. All she wanted to do was go home—see her father and brother again. They were all she had left in the world. If only Noah...

Rubina cried harder.

"Duchessa, we must hurry."

She tried to swallow a lump in her throat, but it was too dry. She let her gaze meet his again and voiced her fear. "Are you real?"

He nodded. "I assure you, I am. Can you walk?"

"I'm so weak..."

"We will go slowly. I will carry you if I must."

He helped Rubina to her feet and led her to the open door. She was about to leave her prison. How long had she been locked away from the world?

"Why are you helping me?"

"I work for your brother, Conte Leone." They made their way down the long hallway. He stopped at the top of the stone stairway. "My name is Arturo."

"Damian sent you?"

Her family still believed she lived? Why had it taken them so long to find her? Paolo insisted the world believed her dead—as dead as her husband. No more Duke and Duchess of Huntly—no more beautiful love story.

"I'm afraid not." He lifted her up into his arms. "Everyone believes you are dead. I'm here on a different mission. It's a miracle I learned of your existence."

"Grazie." Rubina hugged him. Her whole body

shook with the weight of her emotions. "I feared I'd die locked in that room."

"No need for thanks. I'd do it for anyone." His mouth formed a firm straight line. "What the Duca d'Sordillo was doing to you was wrong."

Rubina didn't want to think about Paolo. She just wanted to get as far away from him as possible. Maybe she'd return to England... She loved her home. Italy still held a special place in her heart, but it also filled her with terror. If she had never argued with Noah, Paolo wouldn't have been able to hold her captive. Her only intent had been to return to Naples and visit her father. As soon as she stepped onto the ship heading toward Italy, Paolo's men had seized her. They took her to his ship and locked her inside. Somehow, he arranged to have the ship she'd been on to sink into the ocean's blue depths—sealing the belief of her death.

"If you're not here to rescue me, then what are you doing in Duca di'Sordillo's home?"

"He is believed to have ties to the Mafioso."

Arturo set her down and scanned the room. He pulled her hand into his and led her outside. They stopped in front of a carriage, and he helped her inside. Once Rubina was safely seated, he flicked the reigns to get the horses moving.

"Somehow it doesn't surprise me. He's an evil man—and evidently a mastermind in the criminal underworld."

Arturo nodded. "That's what we believed. We had no idea the extent of his criminal activities. Conte Leone sent me to investigate. If he'd known you were here, he would have come himself and ripped Duca d'Sordillo apart."

Rubina didn't doubt it for a minute. Damian was ruthless when he needed to be. He had a high power seat in the government. He hated the Mafioso and sought to eradicate them from Italy. It was turning out to be a daunting task. The Mafioso themselves were shrouded in secrecy.

"Where are we going?"

"Do you know where you are, Duchessa?"

"Please, call me Rubina," she offered. "I owe you my life. To answer your question—I have no idea where I am or how long I've been here."

Arturo frowned. "This is not good, Your Grace." He shook his head. "You are in Sicily near Palermo. It's been three years since the Conte and your father believed you drowned aboard that ship."

Rubina gasped. "No, so long..."

"Your family—they will be so relieved to find you still live. Thankfully, your brother awaits me in a nearby port. We can escape with him and travel to Naples."

Damian was near? The fates had finally decided to step in and help her. If only they'd done so sooner—she might have been able to save Noah. Pinpricks of pain shot through her heart as a vision of her beloved floated before her. She missed him so much.

Arturo urged the horses to go faster. The wind blew through Rubina's hair. Soon she'd be with her brother again, and she could plot Duca d'Sordillo's death. He would pay for his sins. First she'd need to regain her strength. She would not be able to defeat him being so weak.

"We'll be to your brother's ship soon, Your Grace."

"Thank you. I'm so tired... Maybe I should sleep a little bit." Her head fell forward, eyes drifting closed. They flew open as she gazed over at him. "I thought I told you to call me Rubina."

"Yes, Your Grace, but I cannot. Please, stay awake. We will be there soon."

Rubina fought her body's need for sleep. Once they got to the ship and reunited with her brother she could give in. Arturo assured her it was near. Deep breath in, exhale, if she kept reminding herself, it all would still be true. If this was a dream, Rubina never wanted to wake up. Only one thing would make it perfect: Noah—alive and well.

The carriage came to a halt near a small pier. The night sky was dark as pitch with tiny white stars dotting the black canvas.

"Duchessa, we are here." He nudged her forward. "Come, I'll help you board the ship."

"I don't think I can move, Arturo." Her eyes rolled backward, and her eyelids fluttered shut. "I don't have much strength left."

"I will carry you." Arturo lifted her into his brawny arms.

The warmth engulfing her spread throughout her whole body. She'd been cold for so long. He nestled her, letting her head rest on his broad shoulder. It was so nice to be taken care of.

"I don't know if I can ever thank you enough," she muttered.

"Quit thanking me, Your Grace."

Rubina never would. He saved her from a living hell.

"What do you have there, Arturo?"

Damian! His voice was music to Rubina's ears. Arturo hadn't lied. He'd brought her to her brother. Rubina wanted to cry again, but she held it inside.

"I found your sister, Conte."

"What?" Disbelief etched through Damian's voice. "You lie, my sister drowned aboard a ship several years ago."

"No, Conte." Arturo shook his head, jostling Rubina's head forward. "She lives. Duca d'Sordillo has kept her locked in a room for years."

Rubina lifted her head and met eyes that matched her own. In the moonlight, his silver-gray irises glowed in front of her. Damian gasped. "*Dio mio*, it's true..."

"Hello, brother."

Damian rushed forward and pulled Rubina out of Arturo's arms. His hug so tight breathing became difficult. "I can't believe you're here. If I'd known..."

"I know, please, I can't breathe."

Damian let her go, never once taking his gaze off of her. She understood because it all seemed like a dream to her too.

"Rue, oh God—Noah. How are we going to tell him?" Damian rubbed his hands over his face. "He is about to get the shock of his life. We must get to him fast."

"What?" Rubina gasped. "Noah lives? Paolo told me he murdered him."

"I assure you, your husband is alive and well." Damian nodded. He paced back and forth in front of her. His agitation making her nervous. "There's something you should know... He's set to remarry."

"No..."

Noah was hers. No other woman would lay claim to him. She had to get to London and reclaim her husband. How dare he move on when she suffered so much? She'd believed he was dead, and still she didn't give in to Paolo. When she got there, Noah would rue the day he'd ever thought to replace her.

ABOUT THE AUTHOR

USA TODAY Bestselling author, DAWN BROWER writes both historical and contemporary romance. There are always stories inside her head; she just never thought she could make them come to life. That creativity has finally found an outlet.

Growing up she was the only girl out of six children. She is a single mother of two teenage boys; there is never a dull moment in her life. Reading books is her favorite hobby and she loves all genres.

Earl of Harrington

A Lady Hoyden's Secret

One Wicked Kiss

Earl In Trouble

All the Ladies Love Coventry

Marsden Descendants

Rebellious Angel

Tempting An American Princess

Marsden Romances

A Flawed Jewel

A Crystal Angel

A Treasured Lily

A Sanguine Gem

A Hidden Ruby

A Discarded Pearl

Novak Springs

Cowgirl Fever

Dirty Proof

Unbridled Pursuit

Sensual Games

Christmas Temptation

Linked Across Time

Saved by My Blackguard

Searching for My Rogue

Seduction of My Rake

Surrendering to My Spy

Spellbound by My Charmer

Stolen by My Knave

Separated from My Love

Scheming with My Duke

Secluded with My Hellion

Heart's Intent

One Heart to Give

Unveiled Hearts

Heart of the Moment

Kiss My Heart Goodbye

Heart in Waiting

Broken Curses

The Enchanted Princess

The Bespelled Knight

The Magical Hunt

Ever Beloved

Forever My Earl

Always My Viscount

Infinitely My Marquess